CHARMED AND D

Clandestine Affairs 1

Zara Chase

MENAGE EVERLASTING

Siren Publishing, Inc.
www.SirenPublishing.com

A SIREN PUBLISHING BOOK
IMPRINT: Ménage Everlasting

CHARMED AND DANGEROUS
Copyright © 2013 by Zara Chase

ISBN: 978-1-62740-443-3

First Printing: September 2013

Cover design by Les Byerley
All art and logo copyright © 2013 by Siren Publishing, Inc.

Printed in the U.S.A.

PUBLISHER
Siren Publishing, Inc.
www.SirenPublishing.com

CHARMED AND DANGEROUS

Clandestine Affairs 1

ZARA CHASE
Copyright © 2013

Chapter One

Raoul watched from his study as Zeke sat stock-still in the center of the paddock. The new stallion stamped and snorted, ran up and down, and generally misbehaved, but Zeke acted as though it didn't exist. Raoul chuckled. He'd give it half an hour before Zeke had the beast literally eating out of his hand.

It took discipline for Raoul to return his attention to his e-mail, which was vastly less entertaining. As usual, there were a dozen requests for help from current service personnel and veterans alike. So far not one of them had held his attention.

"We're not a fucking marriage agency," he grunted, reading and deleting a serving soldier's rambling suspicions about his wife's behavior.

Not for the first time, he wondered how these people managed to obtain his e-mail address. The Clandestine Investigation Agency didn't tout for business—the clue was in the name, for Christ's sake. And what business it did take on didn't involve helping American forces personnel keep track of straying spouses, lost dogs, and all the other routine crap that seemed to find its way into Raoul's inbox. It was downright insulting. They were way better than that.

"Might as well take out an ad in the fucking yellow pages," he groused, deleting yet another stupid request from a soldier in Afghanistan.

Raoul was about to go outside and join Zeke when his private line rang. That got his full attention. He might not be able to keep his e-mail address under wraps, but few people had his personal number. Raoul punched the speakerphone button.

"Washington," he said curtly. "Something I can do for you?"

"Mr. Washington," said a smoky female voice. "I'm Maddie McGuire. Not sure if you remember me but I'm—"

"Major McGuire's daughter," Raoul replied. "I'm sorry about your father. We didn't get a chance to talk at the funeral."

"Thank you, and thanks for coming."

"It was the least we could do. We held your father in great respect."

"That's a kind thing to say."

"It also happens to be the truth. Now, what can I do for you, Maddie?"

"Well, I'm not sure that you can, but…" She cleared her throat. "Dad left me your number. One of the last things he said to me was to contact you if I ever had any problems. I hope you don't mind."

The woman sounded on edge, which was hardly surprising given that her father had died just a few weeks previously. The funeral at Arlington had been a full military honors affair, and rightly so. Maddie had caught Raoul's eye and he was slow to look away again. For the first time in a hell of a long time a woman had pierced the empty shell that used to be his heart. That was probably because, unlike most women he came into contact with, she hadn't been trying to get his attention. Sadness clung to her, and that was something Raoul could identify with.

Maddie's dad had died in suspicious circumstances, and now he'd been buried she probably wanted to find out what had really happened. If that *was* why she was calling, Raoul wouldn't turn her down. He owed it to her, and to her father, to find some answers.

"I don't mind at all. How can I help you?"

"Well, the truth is, I'm scared. Someone's been following me the past couple of days and it's kinda freaked me out."

Raoul sat a little straighter. Maddie had seemed composed and capable at the funeral—not the sort to scare easily.

"Any idea who, or why?"

"No, but it's something to do with Dad."

"What makes you say that?"

"It has to be. My life's an open book, boring and predictable. No one would have reason to follow me."

"No ex-husbands, lovers—"

"No," she replied curtly.

"Sorry, it had to be asked."

"That's okay. My personal life, such as it is, is in New York, but I'm staying at Dad's house in Falls Church, getting his affairs straightened out."

"Which is where you're being followed?"

"Yes."

"Hmm." Perhaps the military were investigating her father's death, even though he'd been led to believe that they had no reason to follow it up. Even so, why tail the daughter? "Tell me everything that's happened."

"Well, it started a couple of days ago. I'd been out, and when I got back, Dad's house had been broken into."

"Anything taken?"

"Hard to say, but the person who broke in was clearly looking for something specific because Dad's home study was targeted."

"Trashed?"

"No, that's the odd thing. Everything was neat and precise. It took me a while to notice that anything was even amiss."

"Military style?"

"Yes, that's what I thought. There was no sign of forced entry, either."

Raoul had a bad feeling about this. Presumably she was speaking on an open line, but thanks to Raoul's obsessiveness with secrecy, his line was secure. Anyone listening in would get nothing more than an earful of static.

"Did you call the cops?" he asked.

"No, I called the military. They came out but didn't do anything. Just said it had to be kids. They still seem to think that Dad being mowed down by a speeding car was nothing more than bad luck." Raoul could hear the frustration in her voice. "Anyway, I don't see how they could have believed what they told me, about it being kids, I mean, because kids don't do professional burglaries."

That was precisely what Raoul had been thinking. "And now you're being followed?"

"Yes, I've seen the same man several times. A big guy wearing a ball cap and jeans. He doesn't try and hide the fact that he's following me, which is what scares me so much. It did cross my mind to go up to him and ask if there was something he wanted from me."

Raoul rolled his eyes. "Please tell me you didn't do that."

"No, common sense prevailed." He could hear the smile in her voice. "I figured I could either confront him or deliver a swift knee in the nuts to put him off."

"That would probably have made matters worse."

"Right. I figured I could pack up Dad's stuff, put the house on the market, and go back to my life. But then I thought why the hell should I? If Dad was into something he shouldn't have been then I want to know what it was."

"I doubt if he was. Your dad was as straight as they come."

"Yes, I know, that's why I don't understand what's going on."

"It must be something to do with his work."

"That's what I thought, but I have no idea what he was doing since his retirement."

"He must have said something."

"Not a lot. Secrecy was second nature to Dad." She sighed. "Anyway, he spoke highly of you, said if I was ever in trouble I should call you and, well…"

"I hear you. Will you be on this number for the next hour or so?"

"Yes, I'm expecting a realtor later this morning."

"Hang tight. I'll get back to you today."

"Thank you, Mr. Washington. I appreciate it."

"Call me Raoul."

"Raoul," she said in that husky voice that did things for him. "I feel better already, knowing I'm not alone."

"Who was that?"

Raoul hadn't heard Zeke come in, but then no one ever heard Zeke unless he wanted them to. Part Native American, he moved as soundlessly and stealthily as a panther.

"I thought you were working your magic on that ornery stallion."

"Oh him." Zeke flapped a hand. "He's just an ol' pussycat."

"Right." Raoul paused. "That was Maddie McGuire. She has problems."

Zeke hitched his hip onto the edge of Raoul's desk. "Tell me."

Raoul filled him in.

"What was Major McGuire working on before he died?"

"That's what I'd give a lot to know. I'd give a hell of a lot more to know why they aren't taking the break-in seriously when it comes so close on the heels of the major's suspicious death."

"Perhaps they are but don't want Maddie to know."

"Do you really believe that?"

"Nope, which means it's definitely one for us." Zeke flashed a knowing smile. "What makes me think you wanna take this one yourself?"

Raoul thought about Maddie and his cock stirred. That part of him definitely wasn't dead, which made him sorely tempted. Even so, he shook his head. If the time ever came to get seriously involved with another woman, he wouldn't mix business with pleasure. That was the surest way to compromise an operation—hell, he should know.

"Why would I want to do that?"

Zeke sighed. "Just thought you might wanna act like a normal guy for a change instead of burying yourself in the countryside and living like a monk."

"Listen who's talking."

"I, my friend, do *not* live like a monk."

Raoul shot his buddy a look as he mentally assessed his options. "Who do we have in the Virginia area?"

"Maddox and Cameron?" Zeke replied without hesitation.

"Yeah." Raoul reached for his phone. "That would work."

* * * *

Maddie kept herself busy for the rest of the morning, trying not to look out the window every two minutes to see if anyone was watching the house. Talking to Raoul had calmed her, and she was starting to think she'd made a fuss about nothing. She'd been on edge ever since her father's unexpected death, and perhaps her imagination was playing tricks on her.

But…she knew what she'd seen—or thought she had. Could it be that she'd invented reasons to call the attractive veteran? Maddie shook her head, unwilling to accept that she'd become that needy. Okay, the moment she'd set eyes on Raoul at the funeral she'd wanted to speak with him, she'd concede that much. There was an uncompromising attitude about the tough Special Forces veteran that made her feel safe just knowing he was in the same room as her. She'd exchanged a few words with him when he arrived at the wake, but before they had a chance to say anything much, others took his place. There'd been so many people there, old friends of her father's keen to speak with her, that by the time she'd gotten around to the cluster of guys Raoul had been with, he'd already split.

Would Raoul come and check things out for himself? she wondered. No, probably not. Hadn't her dad said that he ran a horse ranch in Wyoming? She swallowed down her disappointment, telling herself it was probably just as well. A man who looked as good as he did probably had women falling all over him. Besides, Maddie was off men, permanently. Life was less complicated that way.

When Raoul called her back a short time later and said someone would be in touch with her—someone other than him—she took it like a grown-up.

"Thanks," she said. "I appreciate it."

"Be careful what you say to anyone about your concerns, especially on an open line," he warned her.

"Now you're really scaring me."

"Scared is good. Scared people stay alert. Don't make any more calls or talk about this with anyone. Wait until my people get there and tell them. They'll know what to do."

"Okay, I can do that."

Maddie carried on sorting through her father's papers, wondering if he'd ever thrown anything away in his entire life. She also wondered if there was something amongst all this stuff that would be of interest to the man following her. Old utility bills definitely wouldn't, she thought, throwing the file into a garbage sack. His financial records would need to be gone through though, so she put those in the pile to keep.

Progress was slow since everything she read invoked memories of happier times. Letters from her mother to her father when he was stationed overseas, drawings Maddie herself had done for her dad when she was still a child, her school reports, which he'd kept in a separate file, invitations to long-forgotten parties... It was heartrending. Her dad had been way too young to die, just like her mom had been. It was a tragic waste. Even so, Maddie focused on the task in hand while she waited for Raoul's associate to call.

After a couple of hours she stood up and stretched, her back aching from so much bending. She glanced out the window and saw an SUV drive past the house slowly—the same SUV that had been past several times already today. Her heart rate accelerated. What were the chances of that? This was a quiet street. There was no reason for people to use it unless they lived here. She knew all her father's neighbors by sight, including the cars they drove. She was pretty sure this person wasn't a resident. She craned her neck, trying to decipher the tag. Damn, she couldn't quite see it because it was covered in mud.

Deliberately?

"Get a grip, Maddie," she said aloud. "There's probably a perfectly rational explanation."

Her phone ringing loudly in the otherwise-quiet room made her jump.

"Ms. McGuire?" a male voice asked.

"Yes."

"I'm Riley, a friend of Raoul's," he said. "I'm in the area and wondered if you had time to meet for coffee."

"Sure. There's a Starbucks in town. Do you know it?"

"I'll find it."

"I can be there in half an hour."

"That'll work. See you shortly."

Maddie hung up, glad that Riley hadn't suggested meeting at the house. She'd spent so much time here alone that it felt as though the walls were closing in on her. Grateful for an excuse to escape, she swapped her dusty jeans for a clean pair, ran a brush through her hair, and winced when she glanced in the mirror and saw how tired and drawn she looked. Oh well, what did it matter? Grabbing her keys and purse she headed for her car, locking the house carefully behind her.

She pulled into the Starbucks lot, wondering how she'd recognize Riley. She wasn't left in ignorance for long. Two men, dressed as casually as she was but with military stamped all over them, got out of a truck and ambled over to her. Instinctively aware that they were Raoul's people, she was obliged to suppress a gasp when she lowered her window and looked directly into the eyes of the first guy. Easily six two, he had thick brown hair that touched the collar of his leather jacket, and the deepest brown eyes she'd ever seen in a man. Right now they twinkled with amusement, presumably because her jaw had literally dropped open. Gorgeous to look at, tough, rugged, and dependable were her first impressions. In other words, he was just the person she needed in her corner right now.

"Hey, you have to be Maddie. Raoul told us we'd know you when we saw you." The man stuck out his hand. "I'm Riley Maddox, and this here is Axel Cameron, at your service."

"Er, good to meet you both."

She shook each hand in turn, wondering if she was hallucinating. Axel was almost as tall as Riley, with a riot of thick blond curls and eyes the color of spring grass. Tongue-tied by their good looks and physicality, Maddie didn't know what to make of it when Riley climbed into the passenger seat of her car.

"Let's talk somewhere a bit less conspicuous. Axel will follow behind in our truck."

"Why? What's wrong with right here?"

"We're cautious by nature." He shot her a reassuring smile, revealing a set of white, even teeth and perfect dimples, for God's sake. "We've booked into the Fairview Park Marriott. Know where it is?"

"Sure."

"We won't be interrupted there." He found the lever to push his seat back, offering more space for his long legs. "Just drive, and if anyone tries to follow us, Axel will make sure we lose them."

"He can do that?"

"Darlin', I don't mean to boast, but there ain't much we can't do when we put our minds to it."

Maddie didn't doubt it. "Okay," she said meekly, putting her car into gear and driving off.

Chapter Two

Riley shot sideways glances at their client as she drove the short distance to the hotel. He'd been away on assignment for Raoul when her father had died and hadn't made it to the funeral. Pity that. He'd thought highly of the major and had wanted to pay his respects. He'd never met Maddie before, but his buddy hadn't exaggerated when he described her as a real babe.

She was also wary and tense, with dark shadows beneath her remarkable eyes. Not surprising, given that she'd just had to deal with the trauma of her father's unexpected death and now someone was poking their nose into the major's affairs, probably frightening her stupid. When they'd first heard about her father's untimely demise he'd agreed with Raoul's opinion that it was mildly suspicious and would probably have left it at that. They couldn't possibly right all the world's wrongs.

In light of Maddie's cry for help, leaving it alone was no longer an option. No one who worked for Raoul believed in coincidences, and the feeling that something wasn't right about the major's death had just been upgraded from questionable to a full-blown certainty. Since leaving the military, McGuire had been attached to one of the many secret government agencies that operated out of Virginia. Riley and Axel needed to find out which one and what precisely he did for them.

"Here we are."

She pulled up in the parking lot, pushed a lock of long brunette hair behind one ear, and focused her gaze on Riley's face. Her eyes, a fascinating shade of blue flecked with silver, were filled with a combination of sadness and anxiety. The urge to comfort her was compelling, but Riley reminded himself this was business and sat on his hands, figuratively speaking.

Business always came first.

"Let's wait for Axel before we go inside."

"He ought to be here, surely?" She glanced anxiously out the side window. "What's keeping him?"

"Aw, honey, don't worry about Axel. He can take care of himself. He had company to deal with, is all."

She opened her eyes very wide. "I didn't see anyone."

"A green SUV followed us from Starbucks. I saw it in the wing mirror. You were concentrating on driving so I guess you missed it."

"A green SUV drove past the house several times this morning." She sounded breathless when she spoke. "I hoped it was nothing but—"

"It's okay, Axel's here now, and he's alone."

They got out of her car and Riley led her to the entrance of the hotel. Axel fell into step beside them.

"The guy realized I was on to him and took off," Axel said cheerfully.

"Did he see your ugly mug?"

"I sure as hell hope so. Unfortunately I couldn't see his." He spread his hands. "Tinted glass ain't playing fair."

Riley snorted. "Tell me about it. Did you at least get the tag?"

Axel shot him a pained look. "Do I look like an amateur? I already phoned it through to Raoul. He'll run it for us."

They took the elevator to the top floor as a concession to Maddie. Normally they'd always use the stairs. Elevators broke down, or people got on with you. Sometimes they were people you'd prefer not to be in a confined space with. Since they'd taken up Raoul's offer to join his unofficial band of investigators-cum-vigilantes, there were a lot of people who would probably prefer not to find themselves at close quarters with Riley and Axel.

"Here we are." Axel opened the door to their suite with a card key. "Home sweet home."

"You guys like your comfort," Maddie remarked, glancing around the sitting room and smiling. "Am I paying for this?"

"Did Raoul mention money to you?" Axel asked.

"No, but I assumed—"

"Then you ain't paying."

"Of course I'm paying! I asked for your help, and you can't work for nothing."

Riley grinned. "We do quite a lot of work for the military, clearing up messes they don't want to get involved with, and they pay top dollar. That means, if there's stuff we want to do for people we respect, we don't have to worry about greenbacks."

"That's kind, but—"

"Talk to Raoul if you're bothered about the money side." Axel walked around the room with a wand-like instrument that he waved over the walls and furniture. "Okay, we're all clear."

"What was that?" she asked.

"Checking for bugs," Riley replied offhandedly. "Like I said earlier, we're a suspicious bunch, often with good reason. Not everyone likes us."

"Okay, honey," Axel said. "Let's sit down and talk about your problems. Can we offer you something to drink before we get started?"

"Coffee would be good."

"Coming right up." Axel picked up the phone and placed an order with room service. He then settled in the chair across from Maddie's, draped his long legs casually over its arm, and smiled at her. "We're real sorry about your dad, darlin'. He was a good man."

"Thank you. Yes, he was."

"Where do you call home?" Riley asked, sitting beside her on the couch.

"New York. I'm a freelance interior designer. New York's where it's at, but as long as I have my laptop and cell phone I can work from just about anywhere. That's why I decided to stay here for a while and sort through Dad's stuff." She managed a wan smile. "There's certainly enough of it to go through."

Coffee and cookies arrived. Riley tipped the server while Axel poured. Once they were alone again, Riley got down to business.

"Raoul mentioned that your father's house was broken into but nothing was taken. Is that right?"

"Yes, as far as I can tell. If someone searched, they did it methodically, like they didn't want anyone to know. And presumably they did search. Why else would they break in?"

Axel elevated one brow. "And the military did nothing about it?"

She shook her head. "They all but implied I'd imagined it."

"Who came?"

"Army detectives."

"CIDC." Riley pondered that one for a moment, wondering why the detective division of the US Army would bother themselves with a local break-in. If he was in a charitable frame of mind he'd tell himself it was out of respect for the late major, but cynic that he was, Riley seldom felt charitable. "Did they do anything about it?"

"No, they just had a quick look around, left me their card, and told me to call them if anything else happened."

"Sounds as though they're expecting it to," Axel said, scowling.

Riley nodded. "Yeah, my thoughts exactly. Did your father have a safety deposit box anywhere?" he asked Maddie.

"I'm not sure. I haven't come across any documentation to suggest that he did." She canted her head. "Funny, the military detectives asked me the same question."

Riley and Axel shared a glance. CIDC obviously knew something was off about the major's death and subsequent events—hence sending in the big guns—but seemed content to leave Maddie in the firing line without sharing what they knew with her. Riley wanted to feel surprised.

Unfortunately he didn't.

"That's something we need to look into," Riley said. "If whoever's tailing you didn't get to it already."

"You think that's what all this is about? Dad has something that he shouldn't?" She stared at Riley, pangs of disillusionment and a dawning anger lighting her expression. "Something that got him killed?"

"It's just a theory," Riley replied easily. "It's early days yet, but we need to explore every possibility."

"Who was your daddy working for here in Virginia since leaving the army?" Axel asked.

"He was with the Geospatial-Intelligence Agency."

"Ah, I see." Axel sent her another warm smile. "The eyes of the nation."

"If you say so." She shrugged. "Personally, I have no idea what they do and knew better than to ask Dad. He wouldn't have told me anything even if I had."

"They look for physical features and geographical activities relevant to American interests anywhere on the planet," Riley told her. "It's a fancy title that covers a multitude of sins, but basically they're an early warning system for terrorist activities, natural disasters, stuff like that."

"The GIS majors in information science," Axel added. "Not sure what that means, but it's how they promote themselves in their recruitment pitches."

"But Dad wasn't a scientist."

"Honey, they have scientific folk crawling out their asses. Your dad would have been a damned sight more valuable to them, what with his experience in the military."

"In decoding information, you mean?"

"Right."

Axel laughed. "Their experts probably can't spell half the places where your dad's been stationed at, much less point to them on a map. There is absolutely no substitute for local knowledge."

"I still don't understand why his work with the GIS should put his life in danger." She straightened the sleeve of her shirt, scowling at it like she bore it a grudge. "And if it did and it's now endangering me, why are they pretending otherwise?"

"That, darlin', is what we're here to find out," Riley said. "And to do that we'll need to help you look through your father's stuff. See if we can find anything to do with a safety deposit box, for starters."

"I haven't come across anything that looks official, but then I wouldn't expect to. Dad believed in obeying the rules. If he wasn't supposed to take his work home then it would stay in the office."

"Unless he found something that wasn't right," Riley suggested. "What would he do then?"

Maddie shrugged. "Report it to the right authorities, I suppose."

"Unless he suspected them of being involved," Axel mused. "Perhaps he wasn't sure who to trust."

"Some sort of cover-up?" Riley nodded. "Wouldn't surprise me."

"He'd want to get all his ducks in a row before making accusations," Maddie said, hair cascading over her face as she nodded vigorously. Riley, feeling an overwhelming need to reach forward and push it aside for her, looked away until the moment passed. "He wasn't one to cast aspersions without being sure of his facts."

"Well then, he would have kept his evidence somewhere safe. Otherwise, why all the interest in him and you?" *And why was he killed?* "You need to think where he might have put it. Did he have secret places? A home safe would be too obvious."

"I'm not sure." Once again she frowned. "Everything's such a mess. He never threw anything away, you see."

"It's untidy?" Axel asked, sounding surprised.

"Oh no, everything perfectly orderly, like you'd expect from a man who'd spent so many years in the military." A tiny smile replaced her earlier frown. "There's just an awful lot of it, that's all."

"Which makes it easier to hide things in plain sight," Riley replied.

"Do we really have to go through every single sheet of paper? It'll take forever."

"Unless you can think of a better plan." Axel sent her one of the full-wattage smiles that almost always got him what he wanted, especially when it was directed at a woman. *Whoa, buddy, stay focused on the job in hand.* "We're here to help."

"Has the house in Falls Church always been your family home?" Riley asked.

"Yes. Not that I spent too much time here as a child. Dad was always being posted somewhere or other, and Mom and I often went along." A shadow passed across her eyes, implying that she'd resented always moving from pillar to post. Riley was aware that a lot of army kids felt that way. "But yes, it's the only place I've ever called home."

"It'll be a wrench to sell it then," Axel said.

"Yes and no." She sighed. "Memories are in one's head, not in bricks and mortar."

"Said like a true army brat." Riley winked at her. "Anyway, we'll check out of here and come back to the house with you. You need us close by, just in case you have any more uninvited visitors, and we'll make ourselves useful by helping with the search."

"I thought you would have met with me there in the first place."

Axel smiled. "If someone broke in and didn't steal anything, they probably planted bugs, hoping to hear something interesting."

"Like your reaction if you found anything to do with their business," Riley added, thinking he probably didn't need to point out that she'd have outlived her usefulness once that happened. She seemed like a smart girl and would join the dots quickly enough for herself.

"If they want me to do the searching for them, why try and spook me?"

"That's just the point. They don't want you involved at all. Presumably they thought you'd be gone as soon as the funeral was over, which is when they would have moved in." Riley shook a finger at her and chuckled. "You're not being very cooperative, darlin'."

"Well, excuse me for breathing."

"Tell you what, babe," Axel said, standing up and stretching. "Riley and I will buy you an early dinner, then we'll go back to your old man's place and start searching."

"What about your booking here?"

"No problem. We paid in advance for one night," Riley replied. "Shall we go?"

Chapter Three

Maddie stared at the two men, wondering what to do. When she'd called Raoul she hadn't expected to be offered round-the-clock protection. She might not be in the military herself, but she was no pushover, either. Well, she lived in New York, so that went without being said. She kept fit and knew how to take care of herself but also valued her privacy. Riley and Axel seemed genuinely concerned about her situation. Unlike the army detectives, they saw human shapes where she'd only sensed shadows.

What were you involved with, Daddy?

Knowing the men believed her eased her paranoia. Even so, the thought of having strangers under the same roof as her twenty-four/seven was unnerving. She'd feel a hell of a lot safer, but would she just be exchanging one type of danger for another? The house was large enough to accommodate them with ease, but that didn't mean there was enough space for Maddie to suppress the misplaced feelings that had stirred within her dormant body as soon as the pair introduced themselves.

It seemed disrespectful to be contemplating sex so soon after losing her father, but the prospect had filtered into her brain the moment she met them, and refused to budge. Despite her self-imposed embargo on relationships, she wouldn't turn either of them down and would have a tough job choosing between them if it ever came to that. They were exceptionally fine specimens of the masculine form—handsome, fit, and smart—and she could sense their interest in her went beyond the professional. She'd already seen every female head in the lobby of this hotel turn to follow their progress and also intercepted an array of envious and malicious glances that were sent her way. She'd have to be blind or half-dead not to react to them in the same way.

But still…

"I don't want to make you nervous, darlin'," Riley said softly, "but I think it's very necessary for us to camp out with you, and deep down you probably do, too. Why else did you call Raoul?"

"We're professionals," Axel added. "You don't need to have any worries about us behaving inappropriately."

It's not your inappropriateness that worries me.

"I guess you're right." Maddie grabbed her purse. "Come on then. Let's go."

If they could remain detached and businesslike then so could she.

"Where would you recommend we eat?" Axel asked as they made their way downstairs.

"There's a decent place on North Washington Street called the Beach Shack," she replied. "The food's pretty consistent."

"Okay, I get to ride with you this time." Axel grinned as he opened the driver's door for her. "Riley can follow on in the truck."

"I live to serve," Riley said with a wry smile.

For the first time since she'd received the devastating news about her father, over two weeks beforehand, Maddie found herself thinking about something other than her family life. She would defy any woman who found herself in her situation not to be distracted. At a table that ought to seat six, Maddie felt crowded by the sheer physicality of the two men flanking her. It was early, but the restaurant was already buzzing, and once again Maddie was conscious of other women checking out Riley and Axel.

Hands off, ladies.

They placed their orders. The guys both drank light beers, as though they were on duty, which she supposed they were. Maddie, now happy to cede responsibility for her problems to them, decided she deserved a large glass of chardonnay. They ordered steaks, she went for fish stew. The guys traded insults with one another and plied her with casual questions. All the time she noticed them constantly checking the place out, watching the door whenever it opened, always on the lookout for trouble.

"You an only child, then?" Riley leaned back in his chair and fixed her with a deep, penetrating gaze that affected her all the way to her pussy. Geez, she needed to get laid! "Didn't you ever feel lonely?"

"Yes to both questions. Mom spent her life supporting Dad's career and being a good military wife. I came along late in their marriage, and I don't think I was part of the master plan." She shrugged. "A bit of an inconvenience, really. Oh, don't get me wrong, I wasn't neglected or anything like that. It's just that they were such a compact unit, always on the same page, and didn't seem to need anyone else. I sometimes felt like an outsider."

"But your mom passed some years ago?" Axel asked.

"Yes, nearly ten years. The big *C.* I was eighteen, but Dad wouldn't hear of me dropping my plans to go to college so I could be there for him."

"No responsible father would ask his child to make that sort of sacrifice," Riley replied.

She shook her head, unable to look at them. "No, I guess he didn't need me."

"I'm guessing your dad fell back on military discipline to keep his life on course," Axel said.

"The army had always been his *other* family," she said, more acerbically than she'd intended. "Mom used to joke that she'd stand a chance if it was another woman she had to compete with."

"People who forge a career in the military often become…well, institutionalized, I guess," Riley said.

"Only other military types truly understand what it takes to live the life," Axel added.

"That's certainly true in Dad's case. We became a lot closer after Mom passed, but I never felt that he needed me, not really."

"How long since he retired?" Riley asked.

"Two years. I made a point of coming home more regularly after that, just in case he was lonely, but he never seemed to be." She grinned. "In fact, he had a lady friend."

Riley's head jerked up. "A local woman?"

"Yes, an army widow." Maddie frowned. "Why? Is it important?"

"Perhaps she knows something about what your father was working on." Axel shrugged. "Pillow talk. It needs to be checked out."

"Oh shit!" Maddie hit her forehead with the heel of her hand. "Talk about an idiot. That idea didn't even occur to me."

"Well, we can soon fix that." Riley smiled at the waitress when she placed his steak in front of him. "Do you get along with her?"

"Oh yes, we're good."

"Come on then," Axel said. "Let's enjoy the food, then we'll set to work at your place. You can help by calling your dad's lady and setting up a meeting for tomorrow."

"Sure, I can do that."

"This steak's good," Riley said, eating quickly.

"Were you guys regular army?" Maddie asked.

"Nah, we're just bog standard retired SEALs." Axel grinned. "There's a lot of us about."

"Ah, that would explain it."

"Explain what?" Riley asked.

"Never mind." She wasn't about to tell them that being part of such a tough, elite force accounted for the way they projected themselves. She suspected that their egos needed no help from her. "Is Raoul an ex-SEAL, too?"

"No, he and his buddy Zeke started Clandestine Investigations together when they left the service. They're both former Green Berets."

"Wow, I really am getting the very best for the dollars your services aren't costing me. I'm flattered." She paused, a forkful of delicious fish halfway to her mouth. "How come two ex-Green Berets finish up ranching horses in Wyoming?"

"There are worse things to do in retirement," Axel said. "We've all seen more than our fair share of wars and atrocities. Besides, that's not all they do."

"Clandestine activities still keep them in touch with their old life?"

"Something like that," Axel replied.

"How did you all get to know my dad?" Maddie asked. "You weren't in the same branch of the service."

"SEALs get to be all over the place. So do Green Berets. We all crossed paths with your dad at various times and were impressed by his leadership qualities," Axel said. "The same can't be said for a lot of top brass in the military, unfortunately. We've seen far too many who get to be where they are for all the wrong reasons."

"Just ask Raoul if you doubt that," Riley said, almost to himself.

"What do you mean by that?"

He shook his head. "Nothing. It's not important."

"Then why mention it?" There was something they weren't telling her, and Maddie's interest was piqued. "And why is Clandestine so…well, clandestine?"

The guys shared a glance. Something passed between them, and it was Riley who eventually answered her. "Raoul was married once."

"Oh, I had no idea."

"Not many people did. His wife was Palestinian. He met her when she worked undercover for the Americans in an effort to broker a peace plan with the Israelis." There was a distant look on Riley's face, implying that he'd digressed mentally. "A certain senior officer who shall remain nameless wanted to use her on a covert operation that Raoul was also involved with. Raoul was firmly against her being part of the setup. He was against the entire plan, come to that. He said it was ill conceived and suspected it had been compromised before it even got off the ground. But the brass pushed ahead, and Raoul's wife was killed in an ambush set by her own people."

"Oh no!" Maddie clapped a hand over her mouth. "That's so sad."

"She was four months pregnant with their first child," Axel added.

"Raoul and Zeke were captured in the same operation when they tried to rescue her and were badly tortured. They managed to escape, not sure how, but I do know Raoul had to be physically restrained when he came face-to-face with the officer who approved the dumb operation." Riley sighed. "Left to his own devices he'd have pulled the bastard's head from his shoulders with his bare hands."

"No one would have blamed him if he had."

"Yeah well, after that Raoul went off the rails for a while."

"How do you mean?" Maddie asked.

"He volunteered for every madcap operation on the books," Axel replied. "It was like he had a death wish. He became a totally focused killing machine, and the army channeled all that anger for its own purposes."

"Typical," Maddie said, rolling her eyes.

"He's a lot better now," Axel said. "He worked through the worst of his anger, but when he came out the other end he decided he'd had enough of the military. He and Zeke got out and bought the horse farm."

"And started Clandestine Investigations?"

"And that," Riley agreed, sighing. "All I can tell you is that there's still a lot of anger bubbling away inside my buddy. I wouldn't like to be that officer if Raoul ever happens to bump into him."

"What happened to him?"

"The officer?" Riley sneered. "He got promoted, of course. He's now a colonel."

"That sucks."

"It's life," Axel replied. "Come on, honey, you're not eating."

Maddie applied herself to her food, thinking about what she'd just been told. "How do you ever get over something like that?" she asked, her heart overflowing with compassion for Raoul. "What Raoul went through, I mean."

"You don't," Riley replied. "You learn to live with it, is all."

The server came to clear their empty plates, sending both men flirtatious glances and ignoring Maddie. They all declined the offer of dessert.

"Guess we should make a move," Axel said.

Riley's phone rang. He checked the display and grinned. "Raoul always know when we're talking about him." He took the call. "Hey, buddy, what's occurring?"

Riley listened, made a few curt comments, and gave Raoul a brief rundown of their progress to date, such as it was.

"Okay, we're heading out to Maddie's house now, and we'll base ourselves there for the duration. We'll let you know if we come up with anything interesting, and you do the same."

Riley pocketed his phone and turned to Maddie. "That car that was following you isn't registered with the Virginia Department of Motor Vehicles."

"Surprise, surprise." Axel chuckled.

"Perhaps they weren't Virginia plates," she said.

"They were," Axel said.

Maddie was confused. "So, what does that mean?"

"Most likely one of the spook organizations based around these parts is keeping tabs on you," Riley said casually. "Anyway, we'll know soon enough."

"How, if the vehicle isn't registered?"

"It had false plates," Axel replied, helping her from her chair. "I'll bet you ten bucks that whoever sent that car will be informed if anyone asks questions about it. Raoul made it easy for them by using a phone line that can be traced right back to him."

Maddie was impressed. "You guys don't miss a trick."

Riley winked at her. "Sometimes it pays to be proactive."

Chapter Four

Riley kept his truck close on the tail of Maddie's Lexus, Axel at its wheel. That was a good move on his buddy's part. The shadows beneath Maddie's eyes suggested that she hadn't been sleeping well. Wiped out emotionally, she was likely still grieving for her father and worried about all the weird stuff that had happened to her over the past few days. Riley didn't blame her for having taken a couple of large glasses of wine with her dinner, but she definitely wasn't safe to drive.

Riley thought about the case as he waited for a signal to change. He'd made light of the information Raoul had come up with, not wanting to freak Maddie out completely, but it had bothered him. Something big was going on here. Houses weren't broken into by professionals, nor were civilians put under surveillance, unless there was a good reason for it. Stuff like that cost big bucks to arrange. If the military had finally decided that Maddie's dad's death was suspicious, they would have told her, wouldn't they?

"Yeah, right," he said aloud, rolling his eyes.

Riley was no longer a naïve recruit and was well aware that the Army CID Command was a law unto itself. If they thought Maddie could be used as bait to get them whatever evidence they needed, they wouldn't hesitate to use her without bothering to ask her permission.

Sorry, guys, that ain't gonna happen.

Riley had only just met Maddie but would be fooling himself if he tried to pretend his interest in her didn't transcend the purely professional. She wasn't the first attractive woman he'd been asked to help since leaving the military, but he'd never even thought about crossing the line with any of them. The possibility had flashed through his mind several times over dinner. There was something about Maddie that broke through his defenses and made him want to go that extra mile for her.

But then what? Riley didn't do relationships—not anymore—and Maddie wasn't the type who'd settle for a one-night stand.

"Don't think about that now," he muttered aloud. "Just concentrate on keeping her safe and getting to the bottom of this mess."

Nothing would happen to Maddie on their watch, Riley would make damned sure of that, but they couldn't hang about indefinitely, waiting for action. Being passive wasn't an option, so Riley figured they'd have to rattle a few cages and see what fell loose.

He started to pay more attention to his surroundings as they drove into a better part of town. The houses became larger, with wider gaps separating them from their neighbors. There didn't seem to be any foot traffic, which helped. Anyone walking around would be easier to spot. The same went for out-of-place vehicles.

Axel pulled the Lexus into the driveway of a house that probably sat on a lot of over an acre. The electronic doors to the garage opened, presumably because Maddie had pressed a button, and Axel pulled the Lexus inside. Riley parked their truck alongside it. There was no sense in advertising their presence here.

The garage door closed noiselessly as they exited their vehicles and Maddie led them into the house through an internal door from the garage.

"Nice place," Riley said, taking a good look around.

They continued to make general conversation as Maddie gave them the guided tour of the five-bedroom home. She'd been warned not to say anything about their suspicions until they'd checked the place out for bugs. Axel extracted his magic wand and found two listening devices—one in her father's home study, the other in the eat-in kitchen. They took it for granted that the phone line was tapped, but since they would only communicate through Riley's and Axel's secure cell phones they didn't bother to remove that one.

Riley and Axel threw their overnight bags into the rooms Maddie assigned to them and got right down to business.

"Okay, babe," Axel said. "The place is clean now. We can talk freely, but don't answer the phone if it rings."

"Oh, but it might be important."

"Are you expecting any calls?" Riley asked.

"Well no, but what if someone wants to talk to me about Dad?"

"We can remove the bug from the phone, but there are other ways that determined people can listen in to landlines," Axel said. "Better not to use it for now. Use our cell phones, and you can give the numbers to anyone you need to keep in touch with."

"Thanks. There's no one right now but I'll bear that in mind."

The fact that she didn't have some man tucked away in New York, anxious to hear from her, made Riley smile with vicarious possessiveness.

"We now know for sure your visitor was here to bug the place," Axel said. "He probably exceeded his orders and couldn't resist having a quick look around, which is why you knew he'd been."

"Whoever sent him will know we found the bugs," Maddie said.

"That's the general idea," Riley replied. "Hopefully it will flush him out. Okay, let's set to work in your daddy's office."

They all moved into the spacious room that had bookshelves lining three walls. There were at least four file cabinets and several separate credenzas full of drawers.

"I see what you mean about neatness," Axel said, opening a drawer to the first file cabinet and gulping when he saw the row of neatly labeled files crammed into the space.

"Precisely, and unfortunately there are no files labeled 'dodgy findings' in any of the drawers."

"That would be too much to ask." Riley chuckled, settling down on his haunches in front of another file cabinet. "What you need to do,

Maddie, is to focus your mind. Get inside your dad's head. If he wanted to hide something where only someone who knows him real well would find it, what place would he choose?"

"Well, I—"

"What mattered to him most in his life?" Axel asked, looking up from a pile of papers he was flipping through.

"My mother and his career," she said without hesitation.

"Too obvious," Riley replied.

"Well, I guess that leaves me. I've already been through all the stuff he kept to do with my school and college work, and there's nothing out of the ordinary."

"Family photographs?" Axel asked. "Have you been through them?"

"No, but wouldn't that be a little too obscure? He didn't know he was going to die, remember."

"Don't forget to call your dad's lady friend," Axel said.

"Oh yes, I'll do it now."

Riley handed her his cell, listening to her end of the conversation with a woman whom she called Claudia.

"She's invited us round tomorrow morning," Maddie said, returning Riley's phone to him.

"Yes, I got that part. Give me her full name, sweetheart."

"Claudia Greenway. Her husband was a major in Dad's old regiment. He died in a roadside ambush in Afghanistan three years ago." She sent him a worried glance. "Why did you need to know all that?"

Without responding, Riley phoned that information through to Raoul and asked for a background check on the woman.

"Was that really necessary?" Maddie asked when Riley hung up.

"Hopefully not, but until we know what we're dealing with, we need to rule out all the obvious suspects."

"I suppose so." She blew air through her lips. "Sorry. I guess I'm a bit on edge."

"No worries." Axel grinned. "You just don't share our suspicious natures, which is kinda refreshing."

They carried out sorting through stuff for another couple of hours, only speaking if anything of consequence came to light, which didn't happen much. Maddie had three piles—things to keep, things to take home and sort through, and things to dispose of. The guys added files to the appropriate piles according to her instructions.

Riley kept Maddie in his line of sight, which was no hardship. Her full breasts strained against the fabric of her top, the nipples pert and clearly visible through the thin fabric, making it hard for him to concentrate on the job in hand. She's pulled her hair into a knot at the back of her neck, giving him a clear view of her profile and the worry lines creasing her brow. The urge to make them go away was driving him crazy and making him damned uncomfortable. He shared a glance with Axel, pretty sure his mind was running along similar lines. They had the same taste in women, and liked to share them, so Riley would bet a year's salary that Axel was as taken with her as he was.

But it couldn't happen. Maddie was in danger, and it was their job to protect her. If they let their guard down and started thinking with their pricks it would be a recipe for disaster.

Maddie stood up, placed both hands on the small of her back and leaned back to straighten out the kinks that had presumably accumulated there. Unfortunately the gesture also pushed her tits out like a written invitation. Riley somehow managed to suppress a groan. Axel was less successful and a strangled oath slipped past his guard. Both men looked away from her, making sure she didn't get to see the bulges in their pants. This was going to be one hell of a tough assignment.

"You look beat, Maddie," he said when he was in control of himself again. "It's getting late. Why not call it a day and get some sleep?"

"Yes, perhaps I will. I haven't been sleeping well."

"You can now," Axel said. "We'll carry on for a bit, make sure the place is secure and act as your guardian angels. You don't have to worry about anything except catching up with your beauty sleep."

She hesitated. "That doesn't seem fair."

"Don't worry about us," Axel said, winking at her. "Beauty sleep won't do anything for either of us."

"Yes, but—"

"Protecting you is partly what we're here to do, Maddie," Riley said. "Go on up. Shout if you need us. Otherwise we'll see you in the morning."

"All right then." She smiled at each of them. "Thanks. I might just take a nice soak in the bath and then turn in. Good night."

"Night," they replied in unison.

They watched the sway of her hips and the movement of her tight ass as she left the room and slowly climbed the stairs. When they were sure she was out of earshot, Axel expelled a deep sigh.

"Shit," he said, thumping his thigh with a clenched fist.

Riley didn't need to ask what he meant. "Yeah, that about covers it."

"How the fuck are we supposed to remain professional?"

"Wish I knew." Riley shook her head. "I don't mind admitting that she's gotten to me. There's something about her. I don't know what it is. We've met enough hot babes in our time, but this one's different."

Axel shot him a look. "Welcome back to the land of the living, buddy."

Is that what was happening to him? Had Riley finally gotten over his disappointment?

"Not sure it's come to that."

"Well, all I know is that Maddie's something else and it's gonna be tough keeping our minds on business when she's around." He paused. "You know, I'm not sure she's actually aware that she oozes sensuality. It kinda gives a guy ideas."

Riley rolled his eyes. "A woman only has to have a pulse to give you ideas."

"Still, someone ought to point it out to her. Seems only right."

"She doesn't seem to have a man in New York."

"That's real strange. Wonder if she's been hurt?"

"Did you notice that she said nothing at all about her personal life? I tried to ask her several times but she deflected my questions."

"I noticed." Axel fell into a chair and gazed off into the distance. "Wonder what she's not telling us."

"Well, I suppose as long as it has nothing to do with her dad, we have no right to pry."

"Yeah, she's the client, and we're supposed to be looking out for her, not devising ways to jump her bones."

"Who's doing that?"

"Tell me you haven't thought about it, Mr. Cool." When Riley looked away and made no reply, Axel flashed a smug grin. "Thought so."

Riley shook his head. "It ain't gonna happen, Axel. Not until we've found out what her daddy was hiding."

"Shit, don't you ever let your guard down?"

Riley grimaced. "Someone has to be the grown-up in this relationship."

"Fuck you!"

"Thanks, but I'll pass. I ain't that desperate yet."

Axel chuckled. "It'll be interesting to hear if Raoul gets any reaction to running that car's plates."

Riley stretched his arms above his head and yawned. "We'll know soon enough."

"So, big thinker, initial ideas?"

"It ain't rocket science. Major McGuire discovered something he wasn't supposed to find and it cost him his life."

"Yeah, I got that part. The question remains, what?"

"Exactly. Unless we can get a handle on what he was working on, we're shooting in the dark."

"The GIS won't give us the time of day." Axel grimaced. "They're either completely out the loop or behind what happened to the major."

"Yeah, I agree."

"What now then?" Axel asked.

"We wait and see if anyone comes calling," Riley replied. "I'm pretty sure no one was watching the house when we arrived, our truck's out of sight, so—"

"So, whoever planted those bugs will want to know why they're no longer working."

"Exactly."

"Then perhaps I shouldn't have frightened the guy in the Jeep off. They'll know now that Maddie's got help."

"I think that'll make them even more determined. Someone wants what the major has awful bad, and there isn't much they won't do to obtain it."

"You think they'll up their game?"

"I think they'll do whatever it takes." Riley flexed his jaw. "We need to take turns keeping watch tonight, buddy. I've got a feeling we'll have visitors sometime soon. You get your head down first and take over from me in three hours."

Axel stood up. "You got it."

Chapter Five

Maddie poured a generous measure of fragrant oil into her steaming bath water and sank into it with a grateful sigh. She closed her eyes, feeling the tension drain out of her along with her aches and pains. The relief of troubles shared was palpable.

She'd never really believed that her father had been careless enough to be hit by a speeding car right outside his own house. No one drove too fast in this residential area. If they did there would have been witnesses because it supposedly took place in broad daylight, but no one saw a thing and the car was never found.

The medical examiner confirmed that her father's injuries were consistent with being hit by a car, but that didn't mean anything. To Maddie's way of thinking, the absence of skid marks and witnesses did. The local police had treated the incident as an unfortunate accident. They seemed reluctant to entertain Maddie's suggestion that her father had been run down elsewhere and then dumped like a sack of potatoes outside his own house. Since she had no plausible explanation as to why it might have happened that way, she'd been forced to let the matter drop.

Everyone spouted the usual platitudes…it was a tragedy…so sad…her father was too young…blah, blah. Maddie had gotten through it all by taking one day at a time. The military listened to her suspicions with polite attentiveness but, to the best of her knowledge, did nothing about them. Maddie came to the conclusion that there was little one woman could do against a solid wall of indifference and would probably have left it at that and returned to her life in New York had it not been for the guy who followed her. And she *knew* he was following her because he wasn't that good at it. Or perhaps he wanted to intimidate her into leaving.

Big mistake!

If he'd been more patient she'd have been gone by now. Now that he'd confirmed her suspicions, she wasn't going anywhere.

Even so, she was both frightened and unsure how to fight back against her faceless pursuers. Calling Raoul had been an act of sheer desperation. If they could kill someone of her father's standing, how difficult would it be for them to arrange another accident for her? Riley and Axel seemed happy to fight fire with fire and had cheerfully upped the stakes. They seemed self-assured, capable, and most importantly, they'd believed her even before they found the bugs that confirmed her suspicions. That meant a lot to her.

Maddie added more hot water to her now-tepid bath, somnolent but lacking the energy to climb out the tub and dry herself off. Hardly surprisingly, her body had come to life since meeting the guys. All the men she met in New York appeared to be either married, gay, or in therapy. It hadn't seemed to matter. Maddie could live without the complication of having a significant other in her life, especially after her last disastrous attempt at happy ever after.

Riley and Axel's arrival was forcing her to rethink that strategy. Only problem was, they didn't seem to be interested in her in that way. They were caring, polite, and flirtatious but seemed to go out of their way to avoid touching her and hadn't crossed the line that transcended the professional.

"Just as well," Maddie said as she pulled the plug, stood up, and reached for a towel.

She dried herself quickly, brushed her teeth, and then slid naked between crisp cotton sheets. Focusing her thoughts on the two hot saviors now sharing this house with her definitely wouldn't help her get to sleep, but her best efforts to redirect her train of thought seemed doomed to failure. She playfully tweaked a solid nipple as thoughts of Riley filtered through her brain. She wondered how much better it would feel if it were his strong fingers doing the tweaking. He'd heaved a few boxes around as they filled them with stuff for the recycling, and she hadn't been able to avoid noticing the way his muscles bulged and flexed, the way the fabric of his T-shirt strained across his broad chest when he lifted the heavy loads like they weighed nothing at all.

Shit, now she was really awake, in all senses of the word. Moisture trickled between her legs and she was sorely tempted to give herself an orgasm. Then perhaps she'd be able to sleep. Her fingers hovered over her throbbing clit, but she withdrew them at the last minute. She absolutely didn't need to fall back on self-induced sex. She wasn't that desperate and could live without it.

She absolutely could!

Maddie ignored her needs, thumped her pillows into a more comfortable nest, and applied her mind to possible reasons for her father's murder—if that's what it had actually been. The guys seemed convinced that something in this house would point them in the right direction and that she would know where to look. As theories went it had merit, but unfortunately she didn't have a clue where to start the search. She also didn't want to disappoint her pro-bono helpers. Proving to them that she could at least think coherently was important.

Maddie drifted in and out of sleep, telling herself not to think about it. Then perhaps it would come to her.

There had to be something.

There *was* something. Something she'd been avoiding because her emotions were still too raw for her to cope with it. She'd managed to convince herself that her father would never pollute the bedroom he'd shared with Maddie's mother for so many years with anything of dubious provenance. In actual fact, the real reason it was off-limits was because she didn't want to intrude on their personal space. In her heart of hearts Maddie had probably always known that the clue, if it existed, was more likely to be in there than anywhere else.

Maddie had only been in her parents' room briefly since her father's death. It was so achingly familiar and yet so empty without either of them in it that she'd run out again without touching a thing. She was aware that one walk-in closet was still filled with her mother's clothes, everything just the way she'd left it. It was like a shrine, and it would be sacrilege to rummage through it, especially when she had no idea what she was actually looking for.

Damn it, Maddie was bone weary, but now the idea of searching that room had taken root she was unable to sleep. The more she thought about it, the more convinced she became that the clue would be hidden in there somewhere. The guys would probably come to that conclusion pretty soon as well, if they hadn't already, and she didn't want them to be the ones who rummaged through her parents' personal space.

"No time like the present," she muttered, pushing back the covers.

Maddie pulled an oversized T-shirt over her nakedness and crept down the stairs as quietly as she could, treading on the edges of the steps to avoid the parts that creaked. Her parents' room was on the ground floor, and she didn't want Riley or Axel to know she was in there. They might offer to help or try sending her back to bed. Neither prospect was acceptable. The task she'd set herself, too long neglected, needed to be carried out in solitude.

She could hear sounds coming from her father's study. One or both of the guys were still going through his papers. Good, with a bit of luck the noise they were making would blanket any sounds she herself might make. She took a deep breath, opened the door to her parents' room, and switched on a low lamp. The familiar aroma of her father's aftershave greeted her, bringing memories flooding back, making her gasp. It was a smell she recognized from her childhood, since Dad had never changed his brand. Knowing she'd never smell it on him again somehow made his death more final than having watched his coffin being lowered into the ground.

Impatiently she brushed tears away from her eyes. This wasn't an auspicious start. Telling herself to get a grip, she focused on where to start her search. Her mother's dressing room seemed like as good a place as any, so she opened the door and flipped on the light. Nothing seemed to have been disturbed, but there was no dust, either. Presumably Dad's cleaning lady had been charged with keeping the shrine in good shape.

Maddie inhaled deeply as a tingle of awareness rippled down her spine, telling her there was definitely something here. All her mother's shoes were stacked neatly in their original boxes. Her mother had a huge collection, shoes having been her weakness. It became a bit of a family joke, her father often accusing her of having a foot fetish. Smiling through her drying tears, Maddie took a deep breath and opened the first box.

* * * *

Riley heard her coming down the stairs. It had to be her. The tread was too light for it to be Axel. He assumed she couldn't sleep and waited for her to join him in the study. When she didn't, he knew she'd be rooting through her parents' room. Riley had wanted to suggest it earlier but sensed she was still too emotionally fragile to handle something so intimate. Going through her dad's papers was one thing—his clothing and personal affects something altogether different.

Well, it seemed she was made of stronger stuff than Riley had realized. The urge to go and join her was strong, but Riley knew she needed space and left her to it. He returned his attention to the mind-numbingly boring stuff he was methodically going through, more convinced than ever that whatever her father had hidden—*if* he'd hidden anything—wouldn't be found in here. Needles and haystacks came to mind. Axel was pretty good with computers but had found nothing suspicious on her father's machine. Besides, Maddie said he only understood the basics and would never know how to hide stuff securely online. He probably knew it wasn't safe, either. Competent teenagers could, it seemed, hack into just about anything they set their minds to—including the Pentagon.

Maddie remained in her parents' room for more than half an hour. Riley heard nothing to concern him, either from that direction or from would-be intruders. The windows were too secure to be forced, and he'd shot the bolts across on the front and back doors, making covert intrusion impossible. If anyone came calling, Riley would hear them long before they got inside.

He jerked upright, alerted by a noise that had nothing to do with intruders. It was a muffled sound coming from inside the house. Motionless, Riley strained his ears, aware now that it was coming from the master bedroom. With a justifiable excuse to check up on Maddie he strode toward the room, pushed the door open, and stopped dead on the threshold. There was just one soft light burning. Maddie, in a transparent T-shirt, was immediately in front of it, huddled in a tight ball on the bed. Surrounded by open shoe boxes, she was crying into the pillows fit to break her heart.

"Shit!" he muttered almost inaudibly.

Riley knew he ought to remain professional and leave her be. She wouldn't thank him for imposing on her grief, but something stronger than his own will deprived him of the ability to behave sensibly, so leaving simply wasn't an option. In two strides he was at her side, pulling her into his arms so she could sob against his shoulder. She blinked when she realized he was there, and then cried harder than ever, her tears soaking through his T-shirt and dampening his skin. Riley stroked her hair and simply let her cry. He didn't know what else to do.

"Sorry," she said eventually, sniffing.

"It's okay. I'm betting it's the first time you've had a good cry."

"Crying doesn't achieve anything."

"Yeah, it does. We all gotta cry sometimes."

She blinked up at him. "Somehow I can't imagine a tough guy like you ever letting go of his emotions."

"That's because you don't know anything about me." Scared of getting onto personal territory, Riley changed the subject. "What brought you down here anyway?"

"I couldn't sleep." She shrugged against his chest, where Riley was still holding her captive. It felt damned good with her body—her virtually naked body—pressed close to his, and he saw no reason to let her go just yet. "I know I said earlier that it would be too obvious for Dad to hide anything amongst Mom's things, but really I was just being a coward."

"I know."

"Thanks."

Riley laughed. "I'm not suggesting you're a coward, but I understand better than you think how hard it is to go through the personal things of someone close to you."

She blinked. "You do?"

"Sure."

"Did you lose someone?"

Riley cursed his stupidity. He'd wanted to comfort her and hadn't thought about what he was saying. He never spoke about his late wife. Years had gone by but it still hurt like fuck. Maddie looked up to him, her long lashes damp with tears, and he knew he'd do just about anything to make her feel better, including revealing a bit more of himself.

"I was married, years ago now. I'd only been in the marines for a short time when she was diagnosed with a brain tumor." He spoke in a distant voice, pretending it was someone else's tragedy. That helped. "It took her a year to die."

"I'm so sorry."

"It's okay. The pain never goes anywhere, but it does get easier."

"How long ago did this happen?"

"Fifteen years."

"And you never found anyone else?"

"I never looked."

"Is that why you became a SEAL?"

"I guess. I didn't originally intend to stay in the service. Stella was an environmental freak, and we had grand plans to get involved with stuff like that together." He rolled his eyes. "Greenpeace, watch out."

"That's a good thing."

Riley managed a bitter laugh. "We were young and idealistic. I don't think we even stopped to consider what we'd live on while dashing from one environmental protest to the next." He held her a little tighter, conscious of her body warmth seeping through her T-shirt—and his. "After she'd gone I needed something to live for—or an excuse to die, I didn't much care which. The bottom had fallen out of my world and I needed someone to tell me what Stella had done to deserve to die so young."

She reached up and touched his face. "At least my parents had a lot of years together. I can't imagine what it must be like to lose someone you love at such a young age."

"I hope you never get to find out."

"How did you meet Axel? You and he seem pretty tight."

"We went through basic training together and hated one another. We competed like fuck to prove who was the better man." Riley managed a proper smile this time. "In the end the competition bound us together. Stella got sick and Axel was there for me. We got drunk together, he listened while I sounded off and helped me pick up my life after she'd gone. I don't think I'd have gotten through without him."

"He seems like a good guy."

"He's one of the best, but don't tell him I said so. I'd never hear the end of it."

She chuckled. "Your secret's safe with me."

"What about you? Is there—"

"Look at all this mess," she said, pointing to the boxes littering the floor.

Okay, she still doesn't want to talk about personal stuff. "What made you decide to start looking in here?"

"I've been putting it off. All my mom's stuff is untouched and I thought...I thought that perhaps—"

"Shush, it's okay."

She was crying again. Riley held her tighter and brushed his lips against the top of her head. Her hair smelt of sunshine and wildflowers. He wound it around his hand and tugged until her head tilted backward. Her eyes shimmered with the remnants of her tears, her breathing hitched, and the air between them was charged with expectancy. Her lips were moist and shiny, and Riley knew he simply had to kiss her—the fuck with being professional.

He lowered his head, shortening the distance that separated them until he became conscious of her breath peppering his face. Triumph streaked through him as he claimed her sweet mouth in a searing kiss. With a small gasp her lips parted beneath his and his tongue invaded her mouth, exploring with swirling passes as he deepened the kiss.

Riley's body was on fire—his cock rock hard and throbbing—a timely reminder that this was a seriously bad idea. Maddie was their client, and Raoul would tear him a new one if he discovered that Riley had crossed the divide. Getting personally involved with a client was a hanging offence, but the feel of her lush body beneath his hands made it hard for Riley to remember why that was so important. He was only comforting her, he told himself. She was upset and was his responsibility. What else could he do?

Yeah, keep telling yourself that and you might even start to believe it.

A needy moan slipped past their fused lips as Riley deepened the kiss. Her T-shirt had ridden up over her bare thighs, offering graphic proof that she definitely wasn't wearing anything beneath it. *Shit!*

Somehow he found the strength to break the kiss and release the hold he still had on her hair.

"Sorry, darlin'," he said, trying to gently disentangle their limbs. "I shouldn't have done that."

All traces of tears had left her eyes, and the sparkle now reflected in them had little to do with being upset. Her arms were locked around his neck and she didn't seem to be in any hurry to remove them. On her knees, her breasts flattened against his chest, she leaned into him and expelled a throaty little laugh.

"I disagree," she said. "It was exactly the right thing to do."

"Even so, you're our client—"

"Are you always on duty?"

"Maddie, this will complicate everything." Even he could hear that his voice lacked conviction. "We need to focus on—"

"Shush!"

A radiant smile lit her features, like she realized the power in their relationship had just shifted her way. Like she was aware Riley couldn't turn her down, not if this was what she absolutely needed. She flicked a finger against the bulge in his pants and his cock jerked painfully within the confines of his jeans.

"Seems to me you're already pretty focused."

"Axel will kill me," he muttered.

"Why?"

"Because we share everything, that's why."

She gasped, causing Riley to suppose that he'd finally found a way to put her off. Instead her eyes glistened, and she canted her head and ran the tip of her tongue repeatedly across her lower lip.

"Perhaps we should wake him up."

Riley wondered if he'd misheard her. "You like to go with two men at once?"

"I've never tried it, but for you two I could be persuaded to give it a go."

Riley knew when he was beat. Laughing, he took control of the situation by grabbing the hem of her T-shirt and whipping it over her head. Then he took his time, simply looking at her. The view didn't disappoint. Her tits were pert and firm, her waist narrow, and even though she was on her knees, he could already tell that her legs were long, slim, and toned. She was goddamned perfect.

Riley removed his own T-shirt and pulled her back into his arms, his bare chest colliding with her soft breasts, the amalgamation explosive. This time his kiss was as hard and demanding as the rest of him. He cupped her ass, pulling it against his cock as he deepened the kiss, feeding from her sweet mouth. Her hands were in his hair one moment, scratching their way down his back the next, matching his increased urgency. He gave her ass an experimental tap. She shuddered and bit down on his lower lip as though she wanted more of the same.

Maddie seemed to think she could take control. Not a chance! Riley broke the kiss, stood up, and removed his jeans and shorts. She watched him intently, eyes widening when she saw the extent of his erection. He fisted it, just in case she doubted what she was in for. Maddie's only response was a sultry, come-hither smile. Riley was more than ready to oblige. He rejoined her on the bed, tossed her onto her back, and pinned both of her hands above her head, holding them down at the wrist with just one of his own hands.

"Normally I'd shackle these so you'd be at my complete mercy," he said softly. "But today we'll just have to improvise."

"Improvisation is good. I like to improvise."

"Do you like it hard, though, darlin'? That's the question."

"I want you to control me and tell me what to do."

Shit, was she offering to submit to him? To Riley it felt as though all of his birthdays had come at once. He knew there was a reason, over and above the visual, that he was attracted to Maddie. Now he knew what it was. She wasn't a sexual prude and, as she'd just revealed, was happy to experiment.

"You got it, babe." He kissed the end of her nose. "But first off I'm gonna lick you all over."

"You are?"

"Mmm. Then I'm gonna fuck you until you beg for mercy. Now's the time to say if you wanna cry 'wolf.'"

"Are you kidding me?" She sent him a sultry smile. "Do your worst, big boy."

Riley felt like a kid let loose in a candy store, wondering where to start. Disliking the predictable, he zoned in on one of her ears, sucking the lobe into his mouth until she squirmed with impatience. He worked his way down her slender neck and lapped at the pulse throbbing at its base, causing her to emit another needy moan. He sucked and nipped his way lower until he arrived at one of her tits. Squeezing the heavy mound with his free hand, he sucked the solid nipple into his mouth and bit at it. She cried out, but Riley didn't need to look up to know he hadn't hurt her. Maddie was a natural and enjoyed receiving pain as much as he enjoyed inflicting it.

Still keeping her hands above her head, Riley moved to the side of her face and dropped the tip of his cock against her lips.

"Taste me," he said curtly.

Her tongue lapped at his foreskin, sucking up the drop of pre-cum that had oozed out. She worked her way down the sensitive underside of his cock until she reached his laden balls, grabbed the hairs on them between her teeth, and tugged. Riley gritted his own teeth and closed his eyes. *Shit, perhaps this isn't such a good idea.* He removed himself from her mouth and pushed her onto her side.

"Keep your hands where they are, darlin'," Riley said, releasing them. "Grab hold of the headboard and prepare for a hard ride."

"I'm ready," she said, almost sobbing the words.

"I know you are."

He also knew he hadn't touched her cunt and that she must be pretty damned desperate for him to do so. Working from behind her, he moistened his forefinger and rimmed her anus with it. She tensed up but didn't try to stop him. Riley slid his fingers lower, to where her upper thighs were slick with her own juices. She'd told the truth. She was more than ready for him, and Riley was in no mood to make her wait. He reached on the floor for his jeans, extracted a condom from his wallet, tore the packet open with his teeth, and rolled the rubber down his length. Then he spooned behind her and slid between her thighs, easily finding her entrance. She cried out when he pushed inside, probably because she was so tight and he was stretching her to the limit.

"That feels so fucking good," he said, closing his eyes to enhance his pleasure as he worked his way a little deeper.

She pushed back against him. "I need you," she said, sounding desperate. "Don't hold back."

Riley chuckled. "Who's holding back?"

With one hand working her clit, Riley went to work. She moved with him until he was entirely sheathed in her tight warmth. It felt like heaven. Riley couldn't remember the last time he'd invested emotion into the act—well, he could, but he didn't want to think about Stella right now. Instead, he'd live for the moment and figure out what it all meant at a more appropriate time.

"Come on, darlin'," he purred in her ear. "Let it go. I can tell you're close."

He worked his fingers across her clit a little harder and she cried out, her entire body spasming as she came. The moment she stilled Riley picked up the rhythm, thrusting hard and deep from behind.

"Now for the main act," he said. "Keep taking it, darlin', I'm so fucking close."

"Me as well." There was surprise in her voice, like she'd never come twice in quick succession before. "It's astonishing."

"Get used to it. Axel and I like to give total satisfaction."

"Riley, I..."

She screamed so loud that Axel must have heard her. On the brink of his own orgasm, Riley couldn't have cared less. He grabbed her hips and thrust into her like a man with ghosts to expunge, groaning as he shot an endless spray of sperm into the condom.

"So much for keeping it professional," said Axel's amused voice from the doorway.

Chapter Six

Axel could sleep anywhere. He'd learned during his time in the service never to pass up on the opportunity to either sleep or eat. His occupation had also taught him to remain alert, even when sleeping. Anything out of place, the slightest disturbance, would find him instantly on his mettle and reaching for a weapon. He'd also acquired the ability to remember exactly where he was without any of the usual disorientation associated with waking up. It was usually some god-awful stink hole at the ass-end of the world where he and his fellow SEALs were waiting, primed and ready to move in as soon as they got the green light.

He woke this time between crisp clean sheets, but the sound that roused him was *definitely* out of place in this house. A woman in the throes of an orgasm? Impossible! Except he knew what he'd heard. Unless Maddie was totally uninhibited when she masturbated, she and Riley must be getting it on.

"Well, well," he muttered, grinning.

He'd known Riley had instantly liked what he saw in Maddie even before they'd talked about it. Hell, what was not to like? It wasn't the first time they'd been attracted to a client, but there was something about Maddie that set her apart. Axel had hope that her allure might break through the rigid standards Riley set for himself—for them both.

He just hadn't expected it to happen so soon.

He pulled on a pair of shorts and slipped down the stairs, careful not to make any noise. Not that it would have mattered because as soon as he reached the master bedroom he realized a herd of elephants could have charged in but the two of them were so into each other they wouldn't have noticed. Alex stood in the doorway for some time, watching them screw one another senseless, a raging hard-on tenting his shorts.

"Axel." Maddie glanced up at him and flashed a thoroughly satiated smile, seemingly unembarrassed by her nakedness. Not that she had anything to be embarrassed about, but he knew how women could be. "Did we wake you?"

"Maddie couldn't sleep," Riley said with a wry grin.

"I was looking through my mom's things to see if I could find anything to help you," she said, speaking at the same time as Riley.

Riley dropped a kiss on her forehead, levered himself from the bed, and disappeared into the bathroom, presumably to dispose of the condom. He returned a second or so later and pulled on his jeans without bothering with his shorts.

"I'll check the perimeter and then get my head down for a while," he said to Axel.

Axel knew it was a deliberate plot to leave him alone with Maddie. How much had Riley told her about their proclivities? Presumably enough to know that she wouldn't freak at the prospect of sharing.

"Any problems you couldn't handle?" Axel asked with a nonchalant smirk.

"His hands are entirely capable," Maddie answered, tossing her head.

Axel chuckled. "You haven't tried mine yet."

She moistened her lips. "Are you offering?"

Riley had already slipped from the room, so Axel sat on the edge of the bed beside her.

"You need to hit the shower and then go back to bed," he said, surprising himself because it was the last thing he actually wanted her to do.

"Are you mad at me…at Riley and me?"

"For starting without me?" Axel shook his head. "Not in the least, but I *am* surprised. Riley never puts pleasure before duty."

"I didn't try to seduce him, if that's what you're thinking."

"I wasn't. Riley only ever does what Riley wants to do."

"He told me about his wife."

Axel elevated his brows. "Now I'm *really* surprised. He never talks about her, not even to me anymore, but he's been hung up about her for way too long. Blames himself for not realizing she was sick. Says if he'd known earlier, they might have been able to do something to save her."

"I don't think it works that way with brain tumors."

Alex grimaced. "Try telling that to Riley."

"About what just happened between us. Are you saying he never goes with women? I find that hard to believe."

"Hell no, he likes to screw as much as the next guy, but he never commits emotionally, which means it's all deeds and little words with him. The fact that he actually talked to you about Stella is a real breakthrough. He's damned crazy to still cling emotionally to her memory, and it's the last thing she'd have wanted." Axel laughed. "Whenever I try to say so, he threatens to pulverize me and tells me to mind my own goddamned business."

"I was upset," Maddie said, pulling her T-shirt back on. "I think he only intended to comfort me, but things got out of hand."

"Only because Riley wanted them to." Axel lifted a hand and pushed a strand of hair behind her ear. "He's got more self-control than a fucking monk."

Maddie flashed a radiant smile. "I'll have to take your word for that."

Axel returned her smile, tempted, so damned tempted. "Yeah, perhaps I could have chosen my words better," he replied softly.

"Why do you stay with him?"

"Someone has to put up with him." Axel chuckled. "A lot of guys who go through the shit we've had to endure finish up hanging out. No one else really understands."

"No, I guess not. I saw the changes in my dad each time he came back from being stationed in war zones, but he never talked about his experiences, either."

"That's half the problem. We have secrecy drummed into us from the get-go, but when it's all over we're told to let it all out because suddenly it's supposed to be cathartic." He shrugged. "By then it's second nature to bottle it all up and the damage is done."

"Do you and Riley live together?"

"Live, work, and play." He waggled his brows at her. "We have a house on Chesapeake Bay and rent out boats to tourists in the summer, take the punters diving, fishing, stuff like that. Well, that and working for Raoul."

She ran her fingers lightly down his forearm. "No special lady in your life, Axel?"

"Not a lot of time for commitment. The service, Riley, and caring for my family have pretty much taken up all my time."

Her T-shirt rode up as she sat cross-legged on the bed, smiling up at him. "Why couldn't your family take care of itself?"

Axel shrugged. "I'm the oldest of four. Mom died when I was twelve. An ectopic pregnancy. She didn't even know she was banged up again until it was too late."

"That's terrible."

"Yeah well, shit happens. After that Dad tried to hold us together, but he lost his job, took to the bottle, and then, one day, he went out for a packet of cigarettes and just kept on walking."

She gasped. "You make it all sound so mundane, but what you're actually saying is that you became father to your siblings when you were still a kid yourself."

"Something like that." Axel wasn't ready to hit her with his life story and changed the subject by nodding toward the boxes littering the floor. "Tell me about all these shoes."

"Well, I figured if Dad *did* hide something important, it would most likely be amongst Mom's things." She flashed a guilty smile. "Mom loved her shoes, a passion that she passed on to me."

Axel glanced at all the boxes again and laughed. "So I see. Any luck?"

"No, and unfortunately I got a bit upset when I found this."

She held out a box a box full of letters that Axel figured had been written by Maddie's father over the years.

"Ah, now I understand." Axel touched her face. "Did you find anything?"

"No, I didn't get that far."

"Why not let me go through them? I can be more objective."

"Would you mind?"

"All part of the service, ma'am."

"Well, if you're sure."

"I'm sure." He tapped her thigh. "Go on, scoot off to bed before I get ideas."

She didn't move. "Riley told me that you like to share."

Shit! "Does the idea appeal to you?" he asked carefully.

She offered him a sultry smile. "You know, I rather think it does."

He leaned in and kissed her. He hadn't meant to touch her because he didn't trust himself to leave it at that, but her lips were so fucking tempting that he couldn't help himself. Still, no way would he fuck her. Not here. Not now. She needed to get used to the idea of getting it on with them both because Axel knew that's what it would come down to. So did Riley, otherwise he wouldn't have given way to temptation and then left him and Maddie alone. She'd given herself to Riley, was clearly equally willing to have Axel, but would she take them both at the same time? Oh, she liked the sound of it, but talk was cheap and mornings after were the time for regrets.

He was totally with Riley when it came to Maddie. She wasn't just another potential conquest but very possibly the element that had been missing from their lives all these years. A disturbing jolt rocked his body as that thought struck home. Was he ready for the change? Axel was as wary of commitment as Riley, or so he'd always thought. But now, before he'd done anything more than kiss Maddie, he was filled with a raging desire to give it a try.

"We're very demanding," he warned her as he broke the kiss. "We'll spank your cute ass, tie you up, bite your nipples, and fuck your ass and cunt simultaneously. You really up for that?"

Her glistening eyes told him that she was. "Absolutely."

"We'll train you so you'll understand how to let the pain transmute to pleasure. It'll blow your mind."

"How about a demonstration?"

"Sexy witch!" Laughing, he pulled her to her feet and patted her ass. "Get back upstairs to your room, hit the shower, and then get some sleep. We have a busy day ahead of us tomorrow. There'll be plenty of time to play after that."

"Have it your way," she said in a tone of wounded dignity that earned her another light tap.

"Oh, I will, darlin'. Count on it."

She blew him a kiss and sauntered from the room, swinging her hips and smiling like she'd learned something about herself in the past few minutes.

Axel remained where he was for a long time after she left him, wondering when he'd developed such a noble streak. His cock had been throbbing with need ever since he saw her and Riley in action, and it had taken a supreme effort to turn her down. He only did so because he figured Maddie wasn't the type to have had sex with two men in the same night before and might regret it in the cold light of day. Axel had already developed deeply protective feelings for her and didn't plan to blow it by pushing her too hard.

"We'd better get to the bottom of her problems pretty damned quick," he muttered.

With a long-suffering sigh, he picked up the box of letters and started to read.

* * * *

Maddie showered quickly and climbed back into bed, expecting not to be able to sleep. To her astonishment it was well past dawn when she next opened her eyes, and she'd slept better than she had for weeks. She stretched and then grinned to herself, her body pleasantly sore as a result of Riley's urgent demands the night before. Athletic sex made for a much better sleeping pill than anything a doctor could prescribe, she decided, wondering if anyone had already patented that particular prescription.

She headed for her shower, aware of muted voices coming from downstairs. Both guys were obviously up already. Well of course they were! Unlike her, military types didn't laze about in bed. She waited for embarrassment at the thought of facing them to kick in, but nothing happened. Why should it? They were all adults, weren't they? If they could treat it as no big deal then so could she.

Maddie pulled on jeans and a sweatshirt, brushed out her hair, and headed downstairs to the kitchen. Something was cooking and the smell caused her stomach to growl.

"Morning, darlin'," Axel said, kissing her cheek. "Sleep well?"

"Like a log, thanks."

Riley's grin was insufferable, like he took personal credit for that situation. "Wonder why?" he said, kissing her also and then placing a huge plateful of fried food in front of her, while Axel poured coffee for them all.

"Er, thanks, but I don't usually—"

"Eat!" Riley commanded.

Maddie bridled at his tone. "I'm not one of your troops you can bark orders at and expect to be obeyed."

"Yeah you are." A wide infectious grin spread across his handsome features. "Which means you need to keep your strength up."

She waved a fork at him. "Has anyone ever told you that you're the most annoyingly arrogant, dictatorial, egotistical—"

"I tell him that all the time," Axel said, shrugging. "It doesn't do any good, though."

Maddie, who really never did have huge cooked breakfasts, found herself eating it anyway. The guys had obviously already had theirs but flanked her, coffee mugs in front of them, as though defying her to leave any.

"I need to save some for the dog," she said, laying her silverware aside when she couldn't eat another bite.

"You don't have a dog," Axel pointed out.

"No, but I'm thinking of getting one." She pinioned Riley with an aggrieved look. "I like dogs. They're loyal, obedient and nonjudgmental."

They both laughed but didn't try to make her eat any more.

"Okay, babe," Riley said as Axel stacked the dirty plates in the dishwasher. "You and I are going to drive over and meet with your dad's friend Claudia this morning. Axel will stay here."

"Why can't Axel come, too?"

"Because no one tried to get in here last night," Axel replied. "We're pretty sure they don't know we're here and that they're probably waiting until they see you go out before coming in to see what's happened to their expensive bugs."

"But Axel might get hurt!"

"He's a big boy, darlin', and can take care of himself."

Maddie wanted to say that she'd have to take his word for that, since unfortunately she had no firsthand knowledge of Axel's actual dimensions. She refrained. They were all business now, and she needed to be as well. One night's hot sex with an even hotter hunk shouldn't mean she'd forgotten all about her father's suspicious death. It had made her feel a hell of a lot better in herself, though, no question about that. The near-constant strain she'd been living with had been replaced with the capricious desire to do madcap things. To make up for lost time and see if these two could really make her body throb to the beat of their particular drum. She was hornier than a high school student on prom night. Just imagining what they could do to her with their large, capable hands and exacting demands had already caused her clean panties to become soaked right through.

Riley's cell phone rang. He checked the display and took the call.

"Hey, Raoul," he said, lifting it to his ear. "What you got for me?" He listened for a while. "That was quick. Yeah, okay, I hear you. We'll be ready for them."

He closed his phone and looked at Axel. "Raoul received a call from a Major Copeland from Army CID."

"He came here and spoke to me after the break in," Maddie said, curling her upper lip disdainfully. "He had a female officer with him, can't remember her name. She was okay, but he was as patronizing as hell, all but suggesting I imagined the home intrusion. I thought he might actually tell me not to worry my pretty little head about it, which would have earned him a swift kick in the balls, the mood I was in at the time."

Both guys laughed. "Well, we've got his full attention now. He wanted to know why Raoul had tried to run the number of the car that was following you."

Maddie widened her eyes. "It was theirs?"

"Yeah. Copeland says they were being thorough and making sure you were okay."

"Bullshit!" Maddie replied.

"What reason did Raoul give?" Axel asked.

"He was as economical with the truth as Copeland was, just saying that Maddie was a personal friend who thought a car was tailing her."

"Which means we can expect a visit from Copeland ourselves," Axel said. "Presumably he doesn't know we're here and will expect to give Maddie a grilling."

"He's certainly welcome to try," she said sweetly.

"Yep, I guess that's what he'll do." Riley indulged in a lazy stretch, providing Maddie with a graphic reminder of his well-defined abs when his shirt rode up. "It also means you were right, babe, and the military do have more of an interest in your father's affairs than they're letting on."

"So why don't they share their suspicions with me?" Maddie asked indignantly. "I have a right to know, especially if I'm in danger. Besides, they scared me, what with that guy following me and everything."

Riley rolled his eyes. "The military don't share with each other, much less outsiders."

"I'm hardly an outsider."

"In their eyes you are," Axel replied. "But don't worry, we're not without a few dirty tricks of our own."

"About Axel staying here while we go and visit with Claudia," Maddie said. "Is that necessary? Can't we assume that if the military are watching me, it was also them that bugged the house?"

"Almost certainly, but it's not safe to make assumptions. We need to know for sure."

"Okay, here's another one. Are you assuming that someone's watching the house?"

Riley nodded. "We can't afford not to consider that possibility. It seems just about everyone else is, including the military."

"Then they'll see you and I drive away together."

"I'll lie down on the floor in the back. If you just open one garage door, anyone close enough to see anything at all won't get a look at our truck."

"Okay then. It seems extreme, but if you're sure."

"Absolutely." Riley stood up. "Are you ready, hon?"

"As I ever will be." She turned to Axel. "Take care."

"Always," he replied with an irrepressible grin.

Chapter Seven

"We're clear now," Maddie said after several minutes. "It's probably safe for you to sit up."

"Have you kept a check on your rearview mirror?"

"Duh, why didn't I think of that?"

"This is serious, Maddie." Riley remained crouched uncomfortably behind the front seat of the Lexus. "You sure you haven't seen the same car behind us?"

"Absolutely sure. I didn't see anyone watching the house, either."

"Doesn't mean it wasn't happening." Riley straightened up and took a good look around as Maddie drove along a main arterial road toward Claudia's suburb. He didn't see anything to excite his interest. "You okay?"

"Yes, I'm fine, just more confused than ever. I really would like to know what Dad got himself involved with."

"Hopefully Claudia will know something."

Riley laid a hand on her shoulder to reassure and as quickly removed it again. He had to remain professional, and feeling the tension in her shoulders didn't help matters. If he thought about their time together last night...well, he'd been doing his darnedest *not* to think about it. It shouldn't have happened was all he knew. The reasons why it had were hard for him to face, so he was avoiding that particular minefield for the time being. One problem at a time.

"Whatever," he continued, "you can bet we'll be receiving a visit from your favorite major before the day's out."

"I can hardly wait."

Riley chuckled. "The poor guy's probably just following orders."

"Yeah, right." She flipped on the indicator, turned right into a residential street, and pulled the car onto the driveway of a neat Cape Cod. "Here we are."

They left the car and ascended the front steps together. Before they could ring, the door was opened by a lady of about fifty. Well-dressed and perfectly made-up, Riley expected her to offer a traditional air-kiss to Maddie. Instead, she engulfed her in a compulsive hug. Riley immediately warmed to her.

"It's lovely to see you." Claudia now held Maddie at arm's length and examined her face. "How are you, dear?"

"I'm bearing up, Claudia, thanks." Maddie extracted herself from the older woman's grasp. "Can I introduce you to Riley Washington, an old friend of Dad's."

"Good to meet you, Ms. Greenway," Riley said, shaking her outstretched hand. "It's kind of you to see us."

"Oh, I always have time for Maddie. And please call me Claudia."

"Thank you, I will."

Clearly bursting with curiosity, Claudia led the way into a cozy family room and offered them coffee. Riley accepted for them both and Claudia excused herself to do the honors. Riley looked around while she was gone. Rooms like this told him a lot about the people who spent time in them, which could sometimes be useful. There were framed photographs lining the mantelpiece, mostly family scenes featuring a younger-looking Claudia and a man often in uniform.

"My late husband and my two children," Claudia said, coming up behind him. "The children are grown and moved away, with families of their own now."

"You must miss them," Riley said, resuming his seat and taking a delicate cup and saucer from Claudia with a nod of thanks.

"They visit regularly." She turned her attention to Maddie. "Now, tell me how you really are."

"I'm doing okay, thanks. How about you?"

Claudia sighed. "The same, I guess. Life goes on."

"Maddie called my buddy and me for help," Riley said when the small talk stalled. "We knew her father, served with him and respected him."

Claudia inclined her head. "I knew you were military," she said. "It always shows in the bearing."

Riley chuckled. "Thanks. I think."

"The thing is, Claudia," Maddie said, leaning forward, "I don't think Dad was hit by a car like they said."

"Oh, but the medical examiner was quite certain—"

"He *was* hit by a car." She paused. "What I should have said is, I don't think it was an accident."

Claudia looked dumfounded. "But why would anyone want to kill Michael?"

"That's what we were hoping you could tell us," Riley said. "His house was broken into just before Maddie called us, and listening devices were placed."

Claudia gasped. "That's a terrible invasion of privacy, Maddie. You must have been terrified, and furious. I know I would be. What have you done about it?"

"Riley and his partner are keeping me company until we get to the bottom of things. We're searching through Dad's things to see if we can find any clues."

Claudia managed a weak smile. "That could take a while."

Riley and Maddie laughed.

"You probably don't know the half of it," Maddie said.

"Did the major intimate to you that anything was amiss with his work?" Riley asked.

"At the GIS, you mean?" Riley nodded in response. "No, he seldom spoke about it."

"Oh well, it was a long shot."

Claudia frowned. "Now that you mention it, he had seemed preoccupied just before his death. I asked him if anything was wrong, but he said no."

Riley wasn't surprised to hear it. If the major's concerns centered on his work, he wouldn't talk about it to a civilian.

"Did you meet any of the people he worked with?" he asked, not holding out much hope.

"No, our relationship was relatively new, and we hadn't been out much as a couple. We were easing into it, not advertising it until we were completely comfortable with one another. My husband didn't die that long ago, and your dad, Maddie…well—"

"I know how he was about Mom. I kept telling him he ought to look for someone else." Maddie shot Riley a sideways glance, as though the comment was aimed at him as much as Claudia. "Dad only told me a few weeks before he died that he'd found someone special." She touched Claudia's hand. "I'm glad he had you, if only for a short time."

"Thank you." Claudia looked suspiciously close to tears. "That means a lot."

"Did he leave any of his possessions here for safekeeping?" Riley asked.

Claudia shook her head. "We hadn't progressed that far."

Damn, Riley had been so sure. "Well, the question needed to be asked."

"You know that he volunteered at the drop-in center for veterans?" Claudia asked after a prolonged pause.

Riley's head shot up. So, too, did Maddie's.

"No," they said together.

"He said he wanted to give something back. Try and help some of the guys who'd lost their way since leaving the military."

"Typical," Maddie said softly.

"Is the center in Falls Church?" Riley asked.

"Yes." It was Maddie who replied. "I think I know where it is. There's a hostel that offers permanent and temporary accommodation according to need, plus a place where vets can drop in for a meal, medical attention, a hot bath, stuff like that."

"How long had he been going there?" Riley asked.

"A few months, I think," Claudia replied. "He found it depressing and yet rewarding, if that makes any sense."

"There was nothing there that caused him particular concern?"

Claudia spread her hands. "If there was, he didn't share it with me."

Riley stood up. "Well, I guess that about covers it. Thanks for your time, Claudia. It was nice to meet you."

"You, too."

Riley handed her a card. "If you think of anything else, or if anything happens to bother you, you can reach me on this number. Don't call the landline. We think...no, we know it's bugged."

"Oh dear, this sounds serious. You will take good care of Maddie, won't you?"

Riley flashed what he hoped was a reassuring smile. "Count on it, Claudia."

The ladies did a repeat hug, Riley shook Claudia's hand again, and Riley and Maddie then left the house.

"Do you think Claudia's in any danger?" Maddie asked anxiously.

"No, she'll be fine."

Riley slid behind the wheel and drove them back to Maddie's.

"You're no longer concerned about being seen?"

"No, if anyone was going to call on Axel, they would have done it by now. You're probably right anyway and it's the military that placed the bugs."

"Then I shall have a few choice words to address to Major Copeland when he deigns to call."

"Save your breath, babe," he said, patting her knee. "He'll just deny it all."

They arrived home to be told by Axel that all was quiet.

"Which means we can expect Copeland sooner rather than later," Riley replied. "The guy in the car would have told him you weren't alone, Maddie, and that Axel frightened him off. I should have thought of that."

"Ah, so you are fallible," Maddie teased.

Riley shot her a look that, if she'd known him better, would have warned her she'd just earned herself a spanking.

"How did it go with Claudia?" Axel asked.

Riley filled him in. "I wanna check out that vets' center after lunch," he said. "I have a feeling about it."

"Oh God!" Axel clutched his chest dramatically. "He's having one of his feelings. This is *soooo* not good."

Maddie laughed. "I'll prepare lunch right away and then we can get rid of him, Axel."

Over sandwiches and salad, the three of them talked about general things. But all the time an air of expectancy that had nothing to do with the case closed in around them. Try as he might—and he *had* tried real hard—Riley hadn't been able to shake the images of Maddie in the throes of sexual release. Something had unlocked inside him as he fucked her—something he wasn't yet prepared to acknowledge. All he knew was that daylight hadn't shaken the feeling or brought the guilt crashing in on him.

He glanced across the table at Maddie, fascinated by the way her thick lashes curled against her cheek and her eyes sparkled as she exchanged banter with Axel. He wanted her—no question. But until they knew who or what had caused the major's murder, they couldn't afford to let their guard down. Even so, Riley's decision to check out the vets' hostel alone that afternoon was a deliberate ploy to give Axel and Maddie some space. It was time to cut themselves some slack and mix business with pleasure.

But it wasn't to be. They'd barely finished eating when the doorbell sounded.

"Showtime," Riley muttered.

He held out a hand to prevent Maddie from opening the door and did it himself. He peered through the spyhole and saw a man and woman in civilian clothes standing on the stoop. They were definitely military—Copeland and his female colleague, presumably. Riley opened the door, blocking their entrance with his body.

"Afternoon. Something I can do for you?"

Copeland flashed his creds. So, too, did his colleague. Riley took his time studying them. The woman was Captain Shirley Mance, and they were both with CIDC.

"Come to collect your bugs?" Riley asked, moving aside to let them in.

"Who are you, sir?" Copeland asked.

"A friend of Miss McGuire's," Riley replied.

"Sent by Raoul Washington?"

It was Riley's turn to dodge a question. He merely shrugged and led the way into the sitting room, where Axel and Maddie awaited them.

"Major, how nice to see you again," Maddie said, heavy on the sarcasm.

"We were just passing—"

"Of course you were."

"We wanted to make sure you were all right and tell you that we're taking your concerns about your father's death very seriously."

Maddie elevated a brow. "The concerns that you told me were unfounded?"

"That isn't precisely what we said."

"Even so, I'm guessing you have no news."

"Unfortunately not."

"Well, as you can see, I'm well protected, so I won't keep you."

"That car you spotted—"

"Would that be the one you didn't bother to tell me about?" Maddie glowered at them. "The one that scared me half to death?"

"It was for your own protection, ma'am," the woman said smoothly.

"But you all but told me I was imagining things." Maddie plonked her hands on her hips. "Why did you break in here and place bugs in my father's house? What were you hoping to hear?"

"There were certain…er, anomalies about your father's death and we wanted to be absolutely sure."

"If you tell us what it is that you suspect, or hope to find," Riley said, "we'll be happy to work with you."

Copeland fixed him with a steely glare. "I can't help you."

"Ditto," Riley replied.

"Leaving aside the fact that you told me there was nothing suspicious about Dad's death," Maddie reiterated, "what right did you have to break in?"

"Did I say we knew anything about listening devices or break-ins?" Copeland asked with an arrogant snarl.

"Don't play word games with me, Major," Maddie replied, clearly seething. "You just all but admitted it."

"Did I?"

Riley hadn't known the man for five minutes but could already understand Maddie's desire to knee him in the nuts.

"If you or your friends have anything concrete to share with us, we're more than ready to hear it," Copeland said.

"I'll bet," Riley muttered.

"Leave me alone, Major," Maddie said, getting right up into his face. "When I needed your help, you didn't want to know. It's too late now."

"You don't seem to understand."

"No, it's you that doesn't understand, so let me make myself crystal clear. If I detect anyone following me, watching me, or trying to bug my house, then I have friends in high places who'll make life damned uncomfortable for you." Maddie was magnificent in her anger. Riley wanted to applaud but made do with sending Copeland a smug half-smile. "Now, get out."

The two investigators turned to go.

"I think this belongs to you," Axel said, tossing the bug he'd extracted from the landline to Copeland, who reflexively caught it.

Chapter Eight

"What the hell's going on?" Maddie asked, sinking into a chair.

"Good question," Riley replied.

Maddie frowned. "I don't get it. If they still think Dad's death wasn't an accident, why go to the trouble of bugging the house and having me followed?"

"Sorry, babe, but I just don't know." Riley fixed her with a thoughtful gaze. "But I have my suspicions."

Riley paced the length of the room, abstractedly rubbing his chin between his thumb and forefinger. Angry as Maddie was with Copeland and his heavy-handed tactics, she found herself easily distracted by Riley's physicality. Lean, hard, and unquestionably male, he and Axel made the spacious room feel crowded. Their taut bodies and not entirely civilized male auras were squashed into a space that was too small to contain them.

Maddie moistened her lips as she continued to enjoy the view. She must be a very bad person because right now she could barely summon up the will to think about her father. Instead she was fascinated by the six-o'clock shadow stubbling Riley's jaw and the way his hair fell across his chocolate-brown eyes as he brooded on her problems. His strong forearms roped with muscles and his long, capable fingers also caught her attention. She shuddered when she recalled just how enthusiastically her body had come to life beneath those skilled fingers the night before. She turned away from him, mortified to think that her feelings must be written all over her face and that she was drooling like a lovesick teenager.

"If they were sure your dad had been murdered," Riley said pensively, "they wouldn't have had to resort to those methods. They could have told you what they were looking for, asked your permission to search the house, and if you'd failed to give it they could have gotten a warrant and gone ahead with the search anyway."

"They're fishing, in other words," Axel added.

"No, it's worse than that." Riley ground his jaw. "They know what's going on, whatever it was your father found out about, Maddie, or at the very least they suspect something. But they don't want the army to be tainted by association."

Maddie scowled. "You mean they want to cover it up? Sweep Dad's death under the carpet and pretend it never happened?"

"Looks that way. We're all posturing around each other right now. I'll show you mine if you show me yours, and all that shit. Basically that means they want to know what we know but won't reciprocate."

"Only problem is," Axel said, "we don't know diddly-squat."

"We'll just have to figure it out then." Riley picked up the keys to their truck. "I'm going to check out that veterans' hostel, see what shakes loose. Play nice without me, children."

He winked at Maddie and was gone.

Maddie's heart rate quickened when she found herself alone with Axel in a house that suddenly seemed too quiet. Something told her that the immediate danger—if there had ever been any—had passed with Copeland's visit and Axel's mind was no longer on business. He fixed her with a penetrating gaze that confirmed her suspicions—a gaze she felt all the way to her pussy. Her nipples solidified and an anticipatory tingle passed through her body. Axel was making it clear that now was the time to collect on his rain check from the night before, if she'd let him.

Like there was any question of her turning him down! Her entire body was on fire with expectation, and the desire to discover a little bit more about the form of loving he'd already described to her was compulsive. His gaze was still fixed on her face, and she met it head-on.

"Come here."

Axel sat himself in the corner of the sofa, one arm dangling casually along its back, long legs stretched out in front of him, and beckoned to her. She walked slowly toward him, her heart hammering at twice its normal rate. As soon as she was within range his arm snaked out and snagged her around the waist, tumbling her onto his lap. She landed with a soft thud, and her arms automatically worked their way around his neck. She buried her fingers in his thick curls, feeling safe and secure again, just as she had when she'd been with Riley the previous night.

"It's playtime," he said softly. "Are you ready for your first lesson?"

"Yes, absolutely."

"That would be, 'Yes, sir,' or 'Yes, master.'"

"Oh, is that right?"

"Hmm." His lips grazed her neck. "We're more used to giving orders than taking them nowadays."

"My problem is that I've never been good at doing as I'm told," she said, biting her lower lip to stop herself from laughing as she got into the spirit of things.

"Oh, you'll do as we ask you, darlin'," he said, chuckling. "You won't be able to help yourself."

"What happens if I don't?"

Axel shook his head, sending his mop of curls dancing across his eyes. "You sure you want to know? It's pretty bad."

"What can be so very bad?"

"Not getting to have any orgasms when you're desperate to come is worse than water-boarding. Trust me on this."

She opened her eyes very wide, conscious of his thick cock pressing into her buttocks. "Not even once?"

"Nope."

She pouted. "That's just plain mean."

"It gets worse," he replied softly. "Instead of getting release you'll have to stand naked in the corner until Riley and I decide you've learned your lesson."

"Hmm, that doesn't sound like much fun."

"Not for you perhaps, but we'll enjoy looking at your sweet ass and those gorgeous tits." He flicked his fingers across one throbbing nipple through the fabric of her sweatshirt. "But your hands will be tied and your legs shackled apart so you can't do anything to make yourself come."

"You seem to have thought of everything."

Axel chuckled. "We've met females who imagine they can take matters into their own hands before."

Maddie's spine stiffened. "I'm sure you're vastly experienced," she said primly.

Axel chuckled and resumed nuzzling her neck. "And if you do as you're told, you'll benefit from all that experience." His hands drifted beneath her sweatshirt and pushed her bra up. His fingers then sank into the soft flesh of her breasts, kneading and caressing like he had a point to prove. "Good girls get to be fucked as often as they can take it."

"That would be…er, nice."

Axel appeared amused by her feeble response. "Baby, you have no idea."

"Then show me, master."

"Ah, you're getting the idea already. That deserves a reward." Axel pinched her nipple hard and pushed his cock against her backside. Maddie groaned. "You like that, darlin'?"

"Yes, sir."

He tapped her butt and tipped her off his knee. "Take your sweatshirt and bra off. I want to look at you properly."

She stood up and removed both items, then reached for the snap to her jeans.

"Leave them!" Axel ordered curtly. "Never do more than either of us asks of you."

"Oh."

Maddie swallowed, feeling exposed and unsure of herself standing half-dressed in front of Axel. He continued to lounge in the corner of the couch, watching her with an intent expression. Not critical or disappointed, she realized, but deeply appreciative, which made her feel better about herself. Unsure what to do with her hands, Maddie allowed them to fall to her sides as she sent a questioning look Axel's way.

"Lower your eyes and bow your head, Maddie. Never look directly at me when we're you're submitting to me unless I tell you to."

Maddie hesitated for a second or two, thought about arguing, decided against it, and dutifully did as he asked. Far from feeling humiliated, a strange sense of freedom spiraled through her. She was fast discovering that she enjoyed being told what to do. She had no idea what would happen next, and anticipation was half the fun.

"Touch your tits for me," Axel said. "Pinch the nipples as hard as you can take it."

Her hands came up and did as he asked. She'd never gotten much pleasure from touching herself in the past, but seeing the way his eyes darkened and the bulge in his pants expanded as he watched her changed all of that. Maddie was already starting to realize that being dominated didn't mean she wasn't the one wielding the actual power. She gasped when Axel unfastened his jeans and yanked the zip down. He wasn't wearing shorts, and a huge erection, thick and pulsating, sprang from the opening. Axel idly toyed with it, his gaze never once leaving Maddie.

"Take the rest of your clothes off," he said.

It took Maddie mere seconds to step out of her jeans and panties. She threw them aside and resumed her submissive position near the wall, eyes downcast. Her pussy was leaking like a drain, juices trickling down her inner thighs as excitement swamped her senses. Would the trickling moisture earn her a punishment? She had absolutely no idea. Axel was still seated on the couch. Chancing a swift upward glance she found that he was watching her intently, rubbing his cock as he did so. He then stood up, stepped out of his clothes, and approached her. This was it. He'd touch her in some way and it would be game on. He was as aroused as she was, so he couldn't possibly hold out, could he?

Axel walked straight past her as though she wasn't there and left the room without offering any explanation. So much for her being irresistible, she thought with a wry smile, humiliation washing through her. What was she supposed to do now? Stay where she was, stark naked, and wait for him to return? Or was she to assume he'd lost interest and go and find something else to occupy her? Damn it, this wasn't so much fun now.

Before Maddie's annoyance had time to flourish, Axel returned clutching a length of rope he'd obviously found in the garage, and other items that she couldn't make out.

"This is to be your first lesson in submission," he said, approaching her. "You have to learn to hold one position indefinitely, until Riley or I are ready for you to do something else. Normally we'd have all the equipment we need on hand. Since we don't, we're gonna have to improvise. Give me your wrists."

She held them out, and Axel bound them loosely together with a scarf he must have found in her room. He then threw the coil of rope over one of the exposed ceiling beams and fastened it to the scarf binding her wrists.

"Raise your arms above your head, babe. Spread your legs but not too wide. I need you to be able to balance on your toes."

She did so, excitement building as Axel adjusted her limbs to his satisfaction. He then pulled the rope so tight that with her legs spread she really could only balance on her toes. She gasped, feeling anxious and yet liberated, completely at his mercy.

"We need a safety word, darlin'," he said in a seductive purr. "If it gets too much for you, use the word and we stop immediately. What word do you suggest?"

"Copeland," she said without hesitation, thinking of the horrible major who'd so patronized her.

Axel laughed. "That'll be easy enough to remember."

Axel tied something over her eyes and her world went dark. Balancing spread-eagled and naked was liberating, exciting, and painful all at once. She wasn't sure how long she could hold the position. She needed a distraction—something to take her mind off the cramping in her toes. As though he read her mind, she sensed Axel moving closer. She could smell the essence of him and actually felt the heat emanating from his body. A piquant thrill ran through her own oversensitized body because at last he was going to touch her.

He didn't touch her. At least not with his hands, but something so delicate it could almost have been a figment of her imagination rimmed one of her nipples. Maddie gasped. How could something so innocuous send such delicious shivers spiraling through her? Presumably because she couldn't see what was coming, couldn't anticipate what he would do next, but already had total faith in his ability to broaden her horizons.

Something was being done to her other nipple, which caused her to forget all about her cramped toes. The contact with one was almost nonexistent, while the other was being pinched so hard it made her eyes water, sending even more sensation to mess with her mind. The amalgamation of tickle and torture was explosive, and Maddie was almost crying with need.

"I don't understand...I think...what— "

"Wait for the pain to transmute to pleasure," Axel said in a soft, commanding voice.

"But it already has."

Shit, it wasn't his fingers pinching her, it was his teeth doing the damage. She relaxed into the pain, trusting him completely, and was rewarded when exquisite shards of intense awareness trickled from her breast and pooled in the pit of her stomach. She wanted to push herself into his mouth and have him suck her nipple far deeper, but she didn't dare move for fear of losing her balance.

The gentle tickling was working its way down her torso, but his teeth continued to attack one nipple. He was inching closer to her throbbing nub. *Please!* She'd beg aloud if she thought it would do any good. Maddie was too desperate to worry about her pride. She restrained herself, somehow knowing that he wanted her to beg, just so he could punish her by making her wait a little longer. Maddie couldn't possibly wait, not another second. She thrust her pelvis toward him without realizing she'd done it. All contact with her body immediately stopped, and Maddie let out a pathetic-sounding whimper.

"Sorry, master," she said meekly.

He didn't answer her, making Maddie feel wretched for having disappointed him. There was nothing she could do now but submerge herself in the moment, waiting, hoping. There wasn't a sound in the room, other than that of her labored breathing. She couldn't even be sure if Axel was still with her, except she assumed he wouldn't leave her tied up like this with no means of escape.

Without warning, she felt that almost nonexistent sensation resume on the top of the cramped toes of her left foot. Her breathing hitched as she waited to see where it would lead. It crept agonizingly slowly up her calf, paying particular attention to the area behind her knee. Hell, it felt so damned good! Maddie had never given much thought to her knees before and certainly wouldn't have classed them as an erogenous zone.

She forgot all about knees when extreme pressure was put on one of her nipples again, sending her into sensory overdrive. How could he be bending to tickle her calf *and* biting her nipple? She gasped when the truth dawned. He couldn't possibly be doing both—not unless he was a contortionist—so he must have attached something to her nipple. She longed to ask him what it was but feared he might remove it if she did. She wasn't prepared to take that chance and remained silent, absorbing the desire that slammed through her without making a sound.

She felt Axel's hot breath on her pussy—just his breath, damn it. Not his mouth or his fingers. It was too much to endure. If he didn't let her come soon she'd expire from frustration. His rich chuckle echoed through the quiet room, almost as though he could read her mind. Not that that would be too difficult, given the circumstances, she supposed. Suddenly she felt his hair against the insides of her thighs and his mouth latched onto her cunt, sucking at her aching nub as his fingers delved deep inside. She probably wasn't supposed to come—make that she definitely wasn't supposed to—without his permission. Knowing it caused the heady sensations rippling through her to multiply tenfold. She struggled to breathe deeply and evenly, hoping it would help her to maintain control. It didn't do much, and Maddie was now conscious of the perspiration peppering her brow and her limbs trembling uncontrollably.

Screw it! It was too hard, her desperate need too powerful for her to fight against it. With a reckless cry she thrust her hips forward as far as her bound arms permitted and orgasmed in his mouth, bucking and thrusting her way to release. It felt *soooo* good. Maddie allowed the heady feeling to stream through her body, not caring about the consequences.

She thought Axel might stop what he was doing because she'd disobeyed him. Hell, she'd never speak to him again if he did. Instead he increased the pressure of his lips, his tongue swishing firmly upward and barely touching her pussy on its return journey. He was an expert at giving cunnilingus, which hardly came as a big surprise.

"Shit," she said, unable to maintain silence. "Don't stop, Axel, I'm still coming."

Chapter Nine

Riley's drive to the veterans' center gave him an uninterrupted fifteen minutes in which to think about the developing case. Under normal circumstances that would have meant using the time to figure out what Copeland had hoped to discover on his fishing trip to Maddie's home that morning.

But circumstances were far from normal, so he didn't go down that route.

He should also have spent the time trying to decide how to play things when he got to where he was going. What questions to ask and why his sixth sense told him the place held clues when all the time he'd assumed the reason for the major's death was connected to something he'd stumbled upon in his work for GIS.

Riley's mind was having none of it. His concentration was shot to pieces, and all he seemed to be able to think about was Maddie herself—about what had happened between them the previous night and how he felt about her in the cold light of day. He should be chasing his tail, trying to tie this case up so they could all go back to their lives. That way he wouldn't have to think of ways to put Maddie off, should another opportunity to get up close and personal arise.

He wasn't doing that because the plain fact of the matter was he didn't want to put her off. She'd gotten beneath his defenses without even trying, and he wanted to explore the depths of her sensuous nature. They'd barely scratched the surface last night. He knew that for a certainty but was pretty sure Maddie didn't. He chuckled. Well, she'd soon find out because Axel would be putting her through her paces right now.

He and Axel always thought alike when they found a woman they wanted to play with, and they always shared. Axel hadn't said anything more about Riley breaking his own rules, crossing the no-man's-land until the boundaries between business and pleasure became blurred. No, old Axel would be feeling smug and vindicated right now. He'd been telling Riley for years that it was time to let Stella rest in peace and move on with his personal life. He and Axel couldn't afford the luxury of a permanent female in their lives, but hell, a bolt of lightning hadn't struck him down because he'd fucked a client. He'd done what he'd done, and all the time this case went on, he'd continue to want a piece of Maddie. Once wasn't enough for him. No, sir, not nearly. Riley knew in his gut that he'd never be able to get enough of Maddie McGuire.

Hell, he was in trouble!

The downside of mixing business with pleasure was walking around with a near-permanent hard-on. It was happening to him again now, just because he'd been thinking about her and that cute little mewing sound she made when she was close to orgasm.

Shit, this isn't good! He ought to have his mind on business. His cock apparently agreed and was thinking about *its* business. It had swelled up inside his pants, making it near impossible for him to move.

He found the vets' center, a renovated warehouse in a rundown part of downtown with no parking facilities. He followed signs to a nearby parking garage and waited for his erection to subside before locking the truck and walking across a narrow street that backed onto the center. Finding the front door, he pushed all thoughts of Maddie and her wild reaction when she climaxed to the back of his mind. There was a small reception area with a notice board filled with job vacancies, notices of meal times, items for sale, classes—all the usual stuff a person would expect.

Riley looked around, waiting for someone to respond to the bell he'd just rung. The place was sparsely furnished with mismatched chairs and tables that had obviously come from Goodwill, yet meticulously clean and tidy. He'd expect nothing else from an establishment run by former military types. Tidiness came second nature. A smell of cooked food reminded him not so fondly of his old mess hall. He smiled to himself. Some things never changed, and that obviously included the quality of the chow in this pseudo-military establishment.

"Can I help you?"

The question was addressed to Riley by a trim senior, dressed in smart casual clothes, his graying hair cut with military precision, his stance upright, shoulders squared as though still on parade.

"Ah, yes." Riley replaced the leaflet on government benefits he'd been perusing. "I sure hope so."

"You don't look as though you're in need of our services," the older man said, "although I can tell you're ex-military."

"Guilty as charged." Riley stuck out his hand. "Riley Maddox, former marine."

"John Reynolds," the other man responded, giving Riley's hand a firm shake as he continued to size him up. "Career solider."

Reynolds was probably being as economical with the truth about his career as Riley was about his own. He seldom told people that he'd been a SEAL. It was definitely *need to know*, and this guy didn't need to.

"This looks like a worthwhile operation, what I've seen of it," Riley said.

"We do our humble best. Never enough volunteers or money, of course. Speaking of which, dare I hope you've come to volunteer? We're always in need of mentors, or just other military types to talk to our people. Only those that have been there themselves can really understand what our veterans go through."

"That's certainly true, and I'm sorry to disappoint," Riley said, meaning it. "I'm just passing through, but I was hoping to pick someone's brain while I'm here."

"What about?"

Riley was a good judge of character and had already decided that Reynolds played with what his British friends would call a *straight bat.* "Major McGuire," he said. "I gather he volunteered here."

Reynolds's face darkened. "What business is that of yours?"

"I'm a friend of his daughter's, and of Claudia Greenway."

"Ah, Claudia. A lovely lady." Reynolds shook his head mournfully. "Dreadful business with the major. Still haven't gotten over the shock. I don't know Miss McGuire. I feel for her, of course, but I feel for Claudia more, to be honest. I served with her first husband. Claudia was devastated by his loss. She finally found some happiness again, and now this."

"Yeah, it sucks."

"Anyway, why has Miss McGuire sent you here?"

"There are a few bits and pieces belonging to her father that she can't find. She wondered if he had a locker here. She's searched everywhere else and is getting a bit upset." Riley shrugged. "You know how women can be about these things."

Reynolds bridled. "Are you saying that—"

"Hell, no, I'm not suggesting that anything's been stolen. These aren't valuable items anyway, just a few things he always had with him but which weren't on him when he died. Nor are they at his home. It's a longshot, I know, but if there's anywhere here…" Riley allowed his voice to trail off, trusting to luck that Reynolds would fill the ensuing silence. He didn't disappoint.

"I'd like to help, but offhand I can't think of anywhere—"

"What did the major do here anyway, just as a matter of interest?" Riley asked.

"He mostly chatted to some of the newer guys, counseled them, I guess you could say. He helped them to adjust, look for work, or just listened to their woes. Sometimes all they need is a sympathetic ear. Uncle Sam doesn't exactly look after his veterans well, but you don't need me to tell you that."

"I certainly don't." Riley flashed a brief smile. "Can I take a look around?"

Reynolds hesitated for a second and then nodded. "I don't see why not." He pushed in a four-digit code and the door to the main part of the building opened for them. "Right this way."

"Thanks," Riley replied.

"Can you believe we've had to add security?" Reynolds asked. "These guys put their lives on the line on behalf of the good old US of A and get ripped off by way of reward. We've had several break-ins recently and decided after the last one that we'd have to do something about it. Not that there's anything to steal, but it's infuriating, and I still have trouble remembering the code."

Riley wondered if it was true there was nothing to steal, or if it had to do with the major's death.

"What was stolen?" he asked.

"Nothing as far as we could tell. That's what makes it so annoying."

"Do you work here full time?" he asked.

"Yes, I'm one of just four who do. I live on the premises, but before you ask, I didn't hear anything when the break-ins occurred, and I was here on both occasions."

Riley nodded, his suspicions all but confirmed. They were professionals.

"How recent was this?" he asked.

"Quite recent. About a month ago and then last week. Anyway, I hold the whole thing together here. I have the fancy title of Operations Director, which is a pseudonym for general dog's body."

Riley presumed he was supposed to laugh and duly did so. They'd entered a large room, dotted with men of all ages. Some were reading, others playing chess or board games, but most were just staring into space.

"This is our day room," Reynolds explained. "We have twenty fulltime residents here, accepted on a basis of need and ability to contribute."

"It must be tough deciding who qualifies."

Reynolds rolled his eyes. "You have no idea. Problem is, half the people we want to help don't want to be helped. They come in for a hot meal and a bath every so often but that's about it."

"And live rough?"

"I'm afraid so."

"How are you financed?"

"Partly by the state. The major was instrumental in shaming them into that. The rest is through donations." He shrugged. "Like I said before, it's never enough."

"I don't suppose it is."

"Come this way. We have a few lockers back here in the staff room, but I'm pretty sure the major didn't ever use one."

Riley was, too, because none of the major's possessions were actually missing. It was just Riley's way of getting the guided tour. They examined the lockers, but none of them bore the major's name.

"Were the lockers broken into during your burglaries?" he asked.

"As a matter of fact they were. They're used by staff members, but no one leaves anything valuable in them and nothing was taken."

"Hmm, I see."

"Well," Reynolds said, facing Riley and crossing his arms over his chest. "I guess that's a dead end, but then we both knew it would be, didn't we?"

Riley spread his hands and grinned. "Damn, you're good."

"Now we've got that out the way, perhaps you'd do me the courtesy of telling me why you're really here."

Riley hesitated, but only briefly. If the answers were here he'd never find them without Reynolds' cooperation. "We don't think the major's accident was actually an accident," he said succinctly.

Reynolds merely nodded. "That doesn't surprise me. A canny man like the major was never going to get in the way of a speeding car. What I don't understand is why you think it has anything to do with this place."

"I don't. I think it far more likely that he found something he wasn't supposed to in his new job and it cost him his life. Army CIDC told Maddie McGuire that it was definitely an accident but have been sniffing around since my partner and I arrived, which kinda confirms that it wasn't."

"I'd say so." Reynolds looked ready to commit a few murders of his own. "How can we help?"

"Did the major spend more time with one person here rather than another?"

Reynolds thought about it for a moment or two. "No, I'm sorry, I can't say that he did. People come and go all the time, you see."

"Did he fall out with anyone?"

"Again, not so far as I know. Everyone liked and respected him."

Riley was neither surprised nor discouraged by his lack of results. If it was something obvious, it would have come to light before now, and he was used to delving in the dark, waiting for things to emerge. He followed Reynolds outside to a relatively small, immaculately kept garden. Several men were working in it.

"The major enjoyed this little oasis."

"The men working here, are they regular employees or residents?"

"Two residents," he replied, pointing out the men in question. "And one employee."

"Can I meet the employee? If the major spent time out here, it's just possible that he might have seen or heard something of interest."

"By all means." Reynolds waved to a man trimming the edges of the lawn. "Pearson, over here a moment."

A large middle-aged man looked up, acknowledged Reynolds's signal, put down his shears, and walked toward them. As Riley watched him approach he experienced a strong tingling sensation down his spine. He had a feeling he knew who this man was. Reynolds introduced Riley as a friend of the major's and Pearson as an Afghanistan veteran, invalided out of the army. Riley noticed then that Pearson was missing three fingers on one hand and had a scar running down the whole of one side of his face, possibly explaining the presence of a ball cap pulled low over his eyes.

"Well, I must be getting on," Reynolds said. "I'll leave you two to chat."

Both men watched Reynolds go. Only when he'd disappeared inside the building did Riley turn on Pearson with a violent scowl on his face.

"Why were you following Miss McGuire and frightening her half out of her life?" he demanded to know.

* * * *

Maddie's body continued to spasm long after he'd sucked the orgasm from her. She balanced completely still, hands bound above her head, and smiled her defiance. She obviously expected a punishment for coming without Axel's permission. And so she should, but the uninhibited way in which she'd let herself go had blown Axel's mind and it was beyond him to chastise her for it.

"You taste gorgeous," he said, kissing her so she could taste her own juices still on his lips.

Maddie was sex on stilts—one of *the* most sensuous women they'd ever come across—and what it had taken for Riley to come alive again. Finally. Axel had thought that they'd have some fun for a while, just as they always did when they found a woman worth sharing, and then move on. Before he'd even fucked her, he was starting to amend that opinion. Perhaps, just perhaps, Maddie was a keeper. Axel shook his head. No, he and Riley didn't do permanent relationships. Besides, the life they led meant they made a lot of enemies, for whom Maddie would become an easy target. No way were they going to place her in danger. Anyway, she was a career girl, with her life and work in New York.

Axel's cock throbbed a painful reminder that it was being neglected. He grabbed a condom from his wallet, ripped the packet open, and suited up. Never one to rush such important things as fucking, today was going to be an exception to that rule. He placed his hands on Maddie's ass, lifted her from the floor, and she wrapped her legs around his torso without him having to say a word.

He could hear the uneven tenor of her breathing as his cock slid into her entrance. He stretched her to the limit, sighing as he slammed all the way home. He didn't introduce himself slowly. He knew she was aroused and more than ready to meet him halfway, so he thrust into her with urgent intent. Her breath was hot against his damp skin as Axel attempted to control the white-hot explosion building inside him.

"That's it, babe. You've got it all now."

He hammered into her pussy like a man on the brink of losing it. Her breasts—one of which still had a clothespin attached to it— rubbed against the abrasive hairs on his chest, adding to his sensory awareness. Being unable to use her hands, Maddie made athletic use of the muscles in her vagina instead. The little witch closed them about his length each time he plundered her body, holding him captive within her silken fist. He removed one hand from supporting her butt and slapped it hard, clearly taking her by surprise. She gasped, but with Axel still inside her, thrusting hard and deep, she obviously worked through the pain because she stayed right with him.

"How did that feel, darlin'?" he asked. "You like being slapped?"

"Yes," she replied breathlessly. "The tingling feels hot and vibrant. It's wild. I like very much."

He chuckled. "Thought you might say that."

Axel slapped her butt again and picked up the speed of his thrusting.

"Come on, babe. Let's do this together."

"Yes. I'm so fucking close, Axel. This is amazing. Fuck me harder." She threw her head back, banging it on the wall without appearing to notice. "I'm going to come for you, Axel. Keep fucking me."

She clamped his throbbing cock within her spasming sheath, causing Axel to almost lose it. He absolutely couldn't hold back for one second longer. She needed to come again so he could. He slapped her harder than before, hoping it would do the trick. She screamed his name and he knew his desperate gesture had been effective.

"That's it, babe. Take what you need from me. It's all for you."

"I am. I can't stop coming." She circled her head, hair falling all over the place as she took her pleasure. "Axel, just keep fucking me."

"Ride it, darlin'." He ground his teeth as hard as he ground himself into her, straining to hold back. "I'm gonna come, too."

He groaned, calling her filthy names as he plundered her cunt. He closed his eyes when his balls pulled together and he shot his load into the condom. Maddie was screaming again, riding yet another orgasm before the aftershock from its predecessor had even faded.

He removed her bonds and the blindfold and carried her back to the couch, cradling her on his lap.

"Let that be a lesson to you," he said, smiling as he kissed her.

Chapter Ten

Pearson shuffled his feet and fastened his gaze on the ground in front of them, saying nothing. Riley waited him out, certain he was right.

"It's not safe to talk here," he mumbled.

"Why not?"

"I get off in half an hour. There's a bar around the corner called Smith's. I'll meet you in there."

Riley could think of all sorts of reasons why that wouldn't work, the main one being that the guy obviously knew something, had been following Maddie and almost certainly wouldn't show. Then Pearson lifted his gaze from the ground and focused it on Riley's face. Riley could see naked fear in his eyes and figured this thing—whatever it was—ran deeper than he'd realized. Pearson appeared to be a tough veteran, not easily intimidated, but something had scared the fuck out of him.

"All right," Riley said, turning away. "I'll keep a beer cool for you."

"You do that. I'm gonna need it."

Pearson went back to work and Riley retraced his steps through the center.

"Did that get you anywhere?" Reynolds asked from behind the reception desk where he appeared to be immersed in paperwork.

"No, but thanks anyway."

Riley decided to give Pearson the benefit of the doubt and didn't stake out the center, waiting for him to leave. Presumably there was more than one exit, and he couldn't cover them all. He left his truck where it was and covered the short distance to the bar on foot. It was now late afternoon, and those getting off work early were already holding up the bar. It was a bit of a dive, cheap and cheerful with dim lighting and a floor that could do with a decent wash. Riley ordered a light beer for himself and a regular one for Pearson. Then he took a seat in a booth that gave him a clear view of the door and sat back to wait.

His cell phone rang. It was Axel, checking up on him.

"How's it going?" he asked.

Riley chucked. "I might ask you the same question?"

Axel's dramatic sigh echoed down the line. "She. Is. Superb."

"No arguments on this end. Anyway, I found the guy who was following her."

"Good work."

Riley explained.

"You need me to watch your back?"

"Sounds like you have more interesting backs to watch."

"She's sleeping. Poor baby, I wore her out." Axel chuckled. "She ain't used to having multiple orgasms, and it's taken it out of her."

"Yeah, I got that part. But to answer your question, I'll be okay here on my own."

"You sure he'll show?"

"He's just walked in now. Gotta go."

Riley pocketed his phone and waved Pearson over. He pushed himself into the opposite side of the booth and nodded his thanks for the beer. Lifting the bottle to his lips, he downed half of its contents in one swallow, watching Riley the entire time.

"Thirsty work in that garden," he said when he put the bottle back on the table.

"I'm sure it is." Riley fixed him with a glare. "Okay, now that we've got the pleasantries out the way, you need to tell me why you were stalking Ms. McGuire."

"Stalking?" Pearson seemed genuinely surprised by the suggestion. "I wasn't stalking her. I needed to talk to her, that's all."

"Ever heard of the telephone?"

Pearson snorted. "Yeah, like that'd be safe."

"Look, what's this all about?"

He hesitated. "I've no idea who you are. I've never seen you before. You could be one of them sent to trick me."

What the fuck? "I'm ex-military, just like you."

"How did you know Major McGuire?"

"I served with him. He was fine man and a great soldier."

"No arguments there." A little of the tension left Pearson's shoulders. "Where did you serve?"

"All over. Wherever there was war, I was usually close by."

"Me, too."

They shot the breeze for a while, talking about the *good* old days. Any lingering doubts about Pearson's character fell away as they exchanged war stories. Pearson was the real deal. It took one to know one. He was a tough guy who was scared, and men who'd seen as much of the ugly side of life as Pearson had didn't scare easily.

"So what did you need to see Ms. McGuire about?" Riley asked again.

"To warn her she was in danger."

"What from?"

Pearson finished his beer and attracted the server's attention. Only when they both had fresh bottles in front of them did Pearson speak.

"I'm all out of options," he said, spreading the hand with just one finger and a thumb remaining on it. "You tell me you're here to help Ms. McGuire, which indicates they've already tried to get to her, so I guess I can trust you. Fuck it, I need to trust someone."

"If you have any doubts about me, call Ms. McGuire." Riley pulled his cell phone from his pocket and laid it on the table between them. "She'll set you straight. And just so you know, you're right about phones. The one in her father's house was bugged. So, too, was the house itself."

"Shit!" Pearson expelled a long breath, fixing Riley with a steady look as he started to talk. "Okay," he said, "here's the deal."

He spoke in a very low voice, his account succinct yet meticulous. Riley didn't think there was anything in the world that could surprise him. He'd seen it all, done half of it himself in the defense of his country and had the sleepless nights to prove it. But what Pearson told him shook him to the core.

His beer remained untouched in front of him, condensation trickling down the bottle as he listened to what Pearson had to say.

* * * *

Maddie fell out of the shower she'd shared with Axel. He wrapped her in a large fluffy towel, swept her into his arms, and carried her to her bed.

"Get some rest," he said, kissing her brow like she was a child. "Who knows what Riley will have to tell us when he gets back? Need to be ready for anything."

"Stay with me."

He chuckled. "Baby, that's the best offer I've had since I can't remember when, but if I did we wouldn't get much resting done."

"It's the middle of the afternoon," she protested. "Why do I need to rest? I never rest during the day."

Axel chucked. "You don't normally do what we just did, or what you did with Riley last night, either. Your body needs time to adjust."

"But what if Riley needs any help?"

"Riley can take care of himself."

"That's what he said about you."

His eyes sparkled with amusement as he perched one naked buttock on the edge of her bed and playfully tweaked a nipple. "Did that clothespin hurt?"

"Hell no!" She shook her head, grinning like a cat who'd overdosed on a vat of cream. "Who would have thought it?"

"Darlin', you have no idea what pleasure there is to be had from everyday household items when they're put to inventive use, but in order to appreciate them you need to—"

"Don't tell me…rest."

"Exactly."

"Talk to me for a while then," she said, running her fingers down his muscled thigh. "Tell me about the siblings you sacrificed yourself to raise."

"*Quid pro quo*, Clarisse," he said, grinning. "I'll tell you mine if you'll tell me yours."

She laughed. "I have nothing much to tell."

"Everyone has secrets."

She glanced away from him. "Not me."

"Okay then, don't tell. I like a lady of mystery."

"You were going to tell me about your siblings."

He hoisted a brow. "Was I?"

"Do they all look like you?"

"How do I look?"

"Like a surfer dude."

"Looks can be deceptive."

"Obviously. There's a very great deal more to you than a hunky body and a laid-back attitude."

"Thanks. I think."

She leaned up on one elbow. "Come on, Axel, I'm curious."

He sighed. "Okay. I was sixteen and found myself the sole guardian of three bewildered kids who couldn't figure out what had happened to their mom and dad and looked to me for everything."

"But you were too young to take on that sort of responsibility."

"Yeah, and what would have happened if I hadn't?"

"Well, I suppose you'd all have been taken into care."

He shot her a look. "Right. And kept together?"

"Ah, probably not."

"Exactly. I was all they had, and there was no way I was allowing us to be separated. So, I simply didn't tell anyone we were alone."

"How did you manage?"

"Not easily. I graduated high school, worked two jobs, the usual."

"You didn't go to college then?"

"Nah, I worked until my youngest sister was out of school, then I enlisted."

She reached up to touch his face. "You make it all sound so easy, but I know it can't have been."

"You do what you have to do. The upside is that both my sisters are now married to decent guys and have families of their own, and my brother…well, he's gonna make it."

"What happened to him?"

Axel looked away and was quiet for a while. "He got in with the wrong crowd. Drugs, run-ins with the law. I thought he was okay. He'd finished school and was working as a trainer at a local gym, so I decided I could take my eye off the ball and think about myself."

"Not before time. What did you do?"

"What I'd always wanted to do. I enlisted. When I came home on my first leave I saw the state my brother was in and ripped him a new one. The idiot was only dealing drugs out of his gym." He still wouldn't look at her. "He cleaned up his act but drifted back to the white powder time and again—"

"He wasn't as strong as you, obviously. I'm guessing not many people are."

"I always felt that losing our parents affected him the worst. He was a third-grader when Dad left, and he never really got over it." Axel shook his head. "Anyway, he's been clean for a couple of years now. He lives with a woman he met in therapy, and they're strong for each other. Besides, he's an adult now, and how he chooses to live his life is up to him. There's nothing more I can do to help him."

"You're a good man, Axel Cameron," Maddie said, moved almost to tears by his casual way of explaining the huge sacrifice he'd made. "I hope you know that."

"And you need to rest."

"I haven't told you mine yet. That was the agreement."

Axel chuckled. "I raised three kids. You think I don't recognize delaying tactics when I hear them?"

She wriggled into a more comfortable position and pouted. "You can't blame a girl for trying."

He wagged a finger at her. "No, but I can punish you for it."

"Yes please!"

Axel roared with laughter, but instead of making good on his threat he stood up, closed the drapes, and blew her a kiss from the doorway.

"I'll wake you when Riley gets back."

"Spoilsport."

"Oh, don't worry. You'll get all the sport you can handle with Riley and me in the house, and that's a promise."

Maddie hated to admit he was right, but she did feel soporific. Soporific, warm, and satiated, physically and emotionally revived, and a whole bunch of other things she'd never experienced before. It wasn't just the mind-blowing sex but the way Axel had opened up to her about his early life, about the sacrifices he'd made for the sake of his sisters and brother. She suspected he didn't often talk about those things, which made her feel privileged. She was also glad he hadn't let her tell hers. Not that she would have done. She never talked about that stuff and would have made something up, but still…

Her eyes fluttered to a close. She'd take half an hour, then go down and keep Axel company until Riley got back.

When Maddie opened her eyes again, over an hour had gone by. An hour that was filled with *the* most erotic dreams. Except they weren't dreams. It was more a case of her subconscious reliving all the things Axel had just done to her. Even so, she absolutely shouldn't be sleeping the day away when the guys were trying to sort her problems for her, even if Axel had insisted upon it. She pulled on a clean pair of pale blue panties and a matching bra and threw a lightweight shift dress over her head. Maddie then thrust her feet into a pair of wedged mules and made her way downstairs.

"Ah, just in time." The kettle clicked off, and Axel placed a mug of coffee in front of her. "Feeling rested?"

"Hmm." She blew on her steaming coffee and took a cautious sip. "Any word from Riley?"

"Yep, he's on his way back and has news."

"What news?"

"He'll be here any minute, and we'll find out together."

* * * *

Riley used the key Maddie had given him to open her front door and was greeted by the smell of freshly brewed coffee. It gave the place a homely feel and calmed him just a little. And he sure as hell needed to feel calm because what he'd just learned from Pearson had knocked the stuffing out of him.

"Hey," Maddie said, looking up from her perch at the kitchen counter when he walked in. "How did it go?"

Riley dropped a kiss on the top of her head, noticing how gloriously satiated she appeared. Leave it to Axel to do a thorough job. It felt odd walking in on a client and kissing her—odd, but kinda right.

Don't go there, Maddox. Riley reminded himself that Maddie might be different enough to have tempted him to cross the divide between business and pleasure, but he still didn't do happy ever after. Nor would he. Not ever.

"You look…er, content," he said, sharing a look with Axel.

"Thanks, I feel remarkably relaxed," she replied. "Which is more than can be said for you."

"I agree," Axel said, frowning. "What gives, buddy?"

Riley sat down and nodded his thanks to Axel when he placed a cold beer in front of him.

"I now know what this is all about," he said, throwing a notebook on the table.

"What, from the guy who was following me?" Maddie asked. "How can you believe him?"

"The reason you knew he was following you is because he wanted to get your attention. He wanted to warn you."

"Then why didn't he—"

"He's a former soldier and works full time at the vets' center. He and your dad got along real well."

"That's my dad's writing." Maddie grabbed the notebook and flicked through it. "Why did this guy…what's his name—"

"Pearson."

"Why did Pearson have it?"

"Your dad asked him to hide it somewhere no one would think to look. He put it in a cupboard in his gardening shed at the center."

Maddie shook her head. "I still don't get it."

"It was Pearson who first caught on to the fact that everything wasn't right at the center. He told your dad and, well—vets are disappearing." Riley ground his jaw, consumed by anger whenever he thought about what he now knew. "Men who've sacrificed everything for this country for precious little reward are being used as guinea pigs for a drug manufacturer."

Chapter Eleven

"You're kidding me!" Maddie cried. "I don't believe it."

"Unfortunately I do," Axel said with less venom. "Let me guess, they're testing guys with post-traumatic stress to see if it can be fixed retrospectively."

"If they were doing that I could almost condone it," Riley replied, standing up and pacing the length of the kitchen. "But this is nothing to do with the army. Well, not directly."

"Shit!" Axel growled. "It's a private drugs company targeting vulnerable vets with nothing left to lose?"

"That's about the size of it. They pick guys with no families or permanent addresses. Guys who live on the streets but are still able to function, offering them big financial rewards for what they describe as little risk."

"They must have to infect them with small doses of the diseases they're trying to find a cure for without knowing how they'll react," Axel said. "The scumbags!"

"How do they get to the guys?" Maddie asked. "It's not as if they can just wander up to them on the streets. They must need to screen them for suitability, or at least get to know something about them first."

"Your father thought he knew how they do it, and we'll get to that in a moment," Riley replied. "As to the operation itself, it's obviously highly illegal and breaks at least a dozen laws I can think of off the top of my head, so they have to be real careful. They need men who have a certain level of fitness, even if they are down on their luck, and who know how to follow orders."

"So military types would fit the bill," Axel said.

"Right. And like I said, they need to have no one who'll start asking awkward questions if they go missing, because that's what happens." Riley flexed his jaw. "They aren't seen again."

Maddie gasped. "These men die?"

"Or become surplus to requirements," Axel surmised. "They can't be allowed to talk about what they've been through."

"It was Pearson who noticed that a few regulars who'd been going to the center for years stopped coming by for a meal, a bath, and stuff like that," Riley said. "And he did ask questions, but no one seemed to know what had happened to them. Then someone paid Pearson a visit one dark night and told him to back off."

"Which, I'm guessing, was a big mistake," Axel said.

"Right again. Up until then he'd just thought the guys had drifted to another state, somewhere warmer for the winter, and would have left it at that. The visit told him different."

"And he told my dad?"

Riley nodded. "Yep."

"How do you know that the men actually die?" Maddie asked.

"Pearson came across a guy he thought had drifted south but who turned up back on the streets here, a babbling wreck. Pearson had served with the guy, knew him well, and took him back to his place. His mind had gone, but in between the ramblings he learned enough to get the gist of what had happened. He'd been taken to a secure facility, kept in isolation, and made to take pills. He was told it would only be for a couple of weeks and he'd walk away with enough cash to make a new start. The guy got suspicious, stopped taking the pills, and managed to break out when he was waiting for an assessment."

"Does he know where he was held?" Axel asked.

"Somewhere in Montana, he thinks. He hopped a train back here…somehow. Once he was back on familiar territory he just kinda withdrew and Pearson couldn't get him to say much more that made any sense. Pearson said he was scared shitless someone would come after him."

"They couldn't afford for anyone to kiss and tell," Axel said with a disgusted shake of his head.

"Is he all right?" Maddie asked. "We should get some help for him."

"Too late for that." Riley absently ran a hand across her shoulders. "Pearson got home from his shift at the center one day and his buddy was gone. So were his few possessions. It was made to look as though he'd taken off, but the place had been broken into. Professionally, same as here, but Pearson knew his buddy hadn't left of his own volition."

"This is big, Riley," Axel said grimly.

"Damned straight it is."

"So how *do* they get to the guys in the first place?" Maddie asked.

"Accordingly to your father's notebook, it's done through an intermediary at the center during the open evenings they have every Friday. No service man or woman is turned away. There's food and all the other services these people require. They turn it into a bit of a party, according to Pearson, and it gets pretty crowded."

"So it would be easy for someone to pick out suitable candidates," Maddie said disgustedly. "Get chatting to them and fix up follow-ups."

"That's the way I see it."

"Can't be easy, though," Axel said. "I mean, these guys talk to each other. How can the person know they'll keep it to themselves?"

"The prospect of easy money, I guess," Riley replied, shrugging.

"Does Pearson have any idea who it might be?" Axel asked.

"No, but it seems your father had a good idea. He was getting close—"

"Which is why he was killed," Maddie finished for him, shuddering.

"It looks that way." Riley resumed his seat beside her and took her hand. "But don't worry, babe, we're gonna get these people. For your dad's sake and to avenge all the vets who've been taken in by them."

"Why would people go to such lengths?" Maddie asked, shaking her head in obvious bewilderment.

"Do you have any idea just how lucrative the drugs business is in this country?" Riley pushed the hair away from his eyes and continued talking without waiting for a response. "America has just over five percent of the world's population but consumes over eighty percent of the world's painkillers."

"Fucking hell!" Axel sounded stunned. "Remind me of that the next time I get a headache and I'll go cold turkey."

"But drug testing is tightly regulated, isn't it?" Maddie asked.

"Right, which is why those out to make a quick buck are prepared to cut a few corners." Riley ground his jaw. "The financial rewards are massive. So is the pressure to come up with the latest new wonder drug, even though there are already plenty of similar cures on the market. So what if a few rundown vets make the ultimate sacrifice along the way? They're expendable. Besides, it's just another way to serve their country, which ought to make them feel real proud."

"So," Axel said. "You've spoken to Pearson and presumably read the major's journal. Does he give any indication as to who might be doing the recruiting?"

"No, that would be too easy, but my guess is someone in the military's pulling the strings."

Maddie gasped. "What, someone here in Virginia?"

"The guy that runs the center told me that a lot of serving personnel volunteer there."

"Yes, but that would be like turning on their own."

"Like I said earlier," Riley replied, "money transcends all codes of honor. Always has and always will for a lot of people."

"Besides," Axel added, "if that isn't the case, why is your friend Major Copeland so keen to bug your house and phone?"

"They know and aren't stopping it?" Maddie looked fit to explode. "They know my father was murdered and won't even admit it or try to investigate?"

"The military doesn't like washing their dirty linen in public, babe," Riley said, squeezing the hand he was still holding. "You know that."

"Yes, but this is…well, it's evil."

"All the more reason to deal with it in-house," Axel replied. "The military is fighting off savage cuts to its budget as it is. It could do without the horrendous press coverage this would generate."

"I suppose so." Maddie swirled a teaspoon between the fingers of the hand Riley wasn't holding. "But we have to do something, guys. We can't let this carry on."

"We could go to the Friday night beano this week, act as volunteers and see if we can sniff anything out," Axel suggested.

"We could, but somehow I think we'd stand out. We're not local, and we'd create suspicion."

"I could go," Maddie said. "No one would suspect me."

"No!" the guys said together.

"Hey, just a minute, I'm a big girl. I can take care of myself."

"So what are we doing here?" Axel asked.

Riley was about to give her chapter and verse on precisely what could happen, when the door bell sounded.

"You expecting anyone?" he asked Maddie.

"No."

"Okay, stay here. I'll get it."

Riley slid the major's notebook into a kitchen drawer, transferred his pistol to the waistband of his jeans, and walked down the hall. He peered through the spyhole and somehow wasn't surprised to see Major Copeland standing on the stoop. This time he was alone.

"Major, to what do we owe the pleasure?" Riley asked, like he didn't already know.

"Mind if I come in?"

"Be my guest." Riley opened the door wider. "We're in the kitchen."

"It was you I wanted to speak to, as a matter of fact."

Riley didn't doubt it. The local rumor mill was obviously alive and kicking because it hadn't taken the major long to hear of Riley's visit to the vets' center, which was obviously what he wanted to discuss.

"We're still in the kitchen," he said in a take-it-or-leave-it tone.

"Very well, if you're sure Ms. McGuire won't—"

"Rip you a new one?" Riley shrugged, almost enjoying himself. "Guess you're just gonna have to risk it."

The two men walked down the hallway in silence. Riley hoped that Maddie would have the sense to keep a lid on her temper in front of the major, justifiable though her anger might be. Until they knew whose side he was on it would be better to play a tight game.

"We have company," he said, opening the door and ushering the major through it before him.

"Well, well," Axel said with one of his slow, lazy smiles. "Why am I not surprised?"

Maddie looked as though she was about to let fly. Riley sent her a warning glare and she settled for a disgruntled look before submerging into a simmering silence.

Good girl! Copeland looked uncomfortable but had the sense not to try and sweet-talk Maddie. Instead he took the chair beside Axel that Riley pointed him to and got right down to business.

"I hear you were at the vets' center today," he said to Riley. "Find out anything I need to know about?"

Riley remained standing and leaned one shoulder casually against the doorjamb, crossing his arms over his chest. "That rather depends upon what you need to know."

"Anything about the major's activities there would be helpful."

"And why would that be?" Maddie asked. "He died in a tragic accident, didn't he?"

Copeland said nothing, and no one in the room made any attempt to fill the awkward silence that ensued. Riley sensed their visitor was trying to decide how much to tell them about his own investigation in order to learn more about theirs. *Good luck with that one.*

"I haven't been entirely honest with you, Ms. McGuire," he said eventually.

"No shit," Axel replied.

"Most of what I do is classified. I couldn't tell you if I wanted to."

"What *can* you tell us?" Riley asked in an effort to move matters along. It was always the same with these pissing contests. Someone had to break first, and obviously the major had weakened his own position by running to them.

"Not much. You guys are civilians now."

"No former serviceman is ever a really civilian," Axel said quietly.

"So I'm told, but—"

"But if you don't want us bumbling around in your investigation then you'd best level with us and trust to luck that we know how to be discreet."

"Oh, I know you do. I checked you both out. You have friends in high places who speak highly of you."

"Good to know," Axel replied flippantly.

"We've always had suspicions about your father's death, Ms. McGuire."

"What!"

Riley moved toward Maddie and placed a hand on her shoulder, sensing that Copeland's calm revelation was enough to make her lose it. She glanced angrily at Riley's hand and attempted to shake it off. It didn't budge. She expelled several deep breaths and he sensed her anger slowly subsiding. Hopefully she realized they'd find out more if they played it cool. He sat beside her and tapped her thigh beneath the table. She gulped down another lungful of air and gave him a reluctant nod.

"It *was* a hit-and-run," Copeland continued. "But it almost certainly didn't happen in this street, and it was definitely not accidental. We haven't stopped looking for the people responsible—"

"Who can't be charged with murder even if you find them," Maddie said in a mordant tone, "because there's no record of any murder having taken place."

"If we find the people responsible, they'll be charged with a lot more than one murder. Trust me on that."

"Is that supposed to make me feel better? Sweep my father's murder under the rug, like it means nothing at all, and get over myself for feeling short-changed."

"Hear the major out, Maddie," Axel said softly.

"I didn't tell you any of this, Ms. McGuire, because I didn't want to endanger you." He held up a hand to prevent Maddie's interruption. "I don't expect you to believe that, but it's true."

"Tell us what you can, Copeland," Riley said, fed up with his pussyfooting around the subject. "Then we just might share what we know with you."

"Fair enough." He sat ramrod straight, presumably formulating what he intended to say, which almost certainly wouldn't be all he knew. "Vets are disappearing off our streets here in Virginia. We believe they're being used for illegal drugs tests and that Ms. McGuire's father found out about it, which is why he was killed."

"Okay, that jibes with our information," Riley said.

Copeland's head jerked backward. "You found that much out already?"

"We're good at what we do," Axel replied.

"You must be. I'm impressed."

"We know vets are being scoped out at the Friday meetings at the center," Riley said, deciding to level with the major but still not completely trusting him. "What we don't know is who's doing the scoping."

"That's what I've been trying to figure out ever since I found out about the scam." Copeland's frustration appeared genuine. "But I've gotta tell you that so far I've got zilch to show for my efforts."

"But you think it's someone who's still serving?" Axel asked. "Someone based around here."

"Yes, but unfortunately that doesn't narrow it down much."

"Any suspects?" Riley asked.

"Not a one." Copeland glanced at Riley. "How did you discover all this? Did she talk to anyone at the center or did you find papers here?"

"Papers," Riley replied. "He kept notes."

"Ah, can I see them?"

"They won't tell you anything you don't already know, and I'm not prepared to name his informant at this stage."

"Ah, so there is someone."

"Apparently."

"We're on the same side here," Copeland said impatiently. "I could get a warrant."

Riley fixed him with a steady gaze. "But you won't."

Copeland backed down first. "Probably not at this stage."

Riley said nothing but knew he'd won that particular skirmish. Copeland was well aware that the papers in question would disappear long before he could execute a warrant and that he'd only get to see them if Riley decided to let him.

"We've been here for just one day and seem to have found out as much as you and your entire team have uncovered in how long?" Axel asked. "Your answer seemed to be to bug this house and let Maddie do all the work for you."

"That's not why we did that. We were worried in case anyone tried to get to Ms. McGuire."

Maddie had been sitting the entire time with one foot tucked beneath her butt, as though the pins and needles she must now have in her foot had distracted her from blowing her top. She straightened up, placed both feet on the ground, and shared a determined glance between the three of them.

"We were discussing ways of finding out who's behind this before you arrived, Major." From her manner it would seem she agreed with the conclusion Riley had just reached regarding Copeland. He might be a jerk who did things by the book, but he wasn't involved with the bad guys. His frustration at his lack of progress was too genuine to be contrived. "I think I ought to go to tomorrow night's gathering at the center and see what shakes loose."

"And we think that's a lousy idea," Axel countered.

"Actually it could work," Riley replied thoughtfully. "There's nothing to stop all three of us being there to protect Maddie. We can keep her in our sights at all times while she schmoozes. "

"There'll be more than three of us, if she's willing to do it," Copeland said eagerly. "I can have a few more of my people there."

"People you can trust absolutely?" Riley asked skeptically.

"There's no such thing as absolute trust," Copeland countered. "But they're good people who've been with me for a long time."

"I'll do it," Maddie said, looking at Riley as she spoke, as though defying him to override her decision.

"We'll discuss it and get back to you," Riley replied.

"Use my private cell," Copeland said, standing up and handing Riley a card. "Don't talk to anyone else about this except me."

Chapter Twelve

Maddie remained at the kitchen table while Riley and Axel saw the major out. She'd been proven right about her father's death, but that didn't bring much satisfaction. She now urgently needed to know who was behind it all, and absolutely nothing would stop her from going to the center tomorrow night to see what shook loose.

She pulled her father's notebook from the drawer where Riley had hidden it and flipped through it, trying to keep the emotion at bay as she scanned pages covered with her father's familiar writing. It was all neat and precise. Unfortunately it was also in some sort of code—dates, initials, places—but thin on content. Presumably the initials related to missing people. She turned another page. Yes, this section was like a diary.

"Spoke to PL today," she read. *"He hasn't seen JB for two weeks. He was excited about something, thought his fortunes were about to change, but wouldn't say what had happened to shake him out of his depression."*

There were a dozen more entries of a similar nature. A dozen? Had that many people really disappeared without anyone noticing? Well, anyone apart from her father and Pearson, that was? Copeland only seemed to have gotten involved as a result of her father's death. Or had he? Maddie wondered about that. Now that she thought about it, he hadn't actually said very much about the length of time he'd been investigating. She'd just assumed…They should have asked him more about that. He probably wouldn't have told them much, but still, it made Maddie sad to think that men who'd given so much of themselves for their country could be so easily forgotten. She owed it to them to do something. If she couldn't help them then at least she could stop other men falling victim to this cruel scam.

"You okay, darlin'?" Axel asked as the two guys rejoined her.

She shot him a look. "What do you think?"

"I'm guessing you're just the tiniest bit pissed. No one can blame you for that, but you need to stay calm and try to see the broader picture."

"How can Copeland's lot do something like that? They're supposed to uphold the law, but instead they just ignore a murder, like it never happened. One of their own, too. Worse, they knew I could be next on the murderer's list, but they didn't think it worth mentioning. The odd car passing the house occasionally was supposed to keep me safe." Maddie ran a distracted hand through her hair and blew air through her lips. "Pleeaaassseee!"

Riley poured her a glass of wine and opened beers for him and Axel.

"Here, have a drink." Riley sat beside her and passed her a glass of chilled chardonnay. "It'll help."

She sent him a disbelieving glare. "You think?"

"I know you're mad, and heaven knows you have every right to be," Riley said mildly. "But have you stopped to consider how your father would want to play this situation if he was here now?"

"My father's not in a position to do anything."

"No, but if he was."

Maddie scowled. "I don't understand."

"Well, if he had to choose between having Copeland chasing his tail, trying to find the car that ran him down when we all know it's probably at the bottom of some damned lake by now—"

"Or," Axel added, tag teaming his buddy, "have him use his resources to carry on with the investigation that got your dad killed in the first place? Which would the major have opted for?"

"Well, I..." Maddie twisted a strand of hair repeatedly around her forefinger, aware what the reasonable answer ought to be but not feeling in a reasonable mood. "Since you put it like that, I guess he'd want to find out who's recruiting the vets."

"Damned straight he would." Riley rubbed the back of her neck with his strong, capable fingers. It felt *soooo* good. How did he know she was rigid with tension and a massage was just what she needed? "You might not like Copeland, but he seems determined to get to the bottom of this mess. That has to count for something."

Maddie relaxed as Riley's fingers dug deeper. "When did you get to be so wise?" she asked, rotating her shoulders and sighing as the knots started to untangle.

"It's a gift," Riley quipped.

"Do you trust Copeland?" Maddie asked. "He's known a lot more about what's going on than he chose to share with us before now. Don't you think that's kinda odd?"

"He thought he was protecting you."

"Or he could be the one doing the recruiting."

"It's possible," Axel said, "but unlikely. He checked us out, but Raoul returned the favor and ran a check on our buddy Copeland. His record is pretty impressive. He doesn't mind making unpopular decisions if that's what it takes to crack a case, and he has a high success rate."

"Besides," Riley added in a lazy drawl, "we have to trust someone. That doesn't mean I won't be watching him closely, though, darlin'. As far as I'm concerned, the only people who are definitely innocent are the three of us in this room."

"Innocent of anything to do with this business anyway," Axel said, waggling his brows.

Maddie caught his eye, and her treacherous pussy actually started to leak as she recalled their earlier activities. Damn it, she wanted to stay mad at them for riding roughshod over her feelings, for making decisions without consulting her first. But it was hard to maintain the moral high ground when she thought about how Axel had tied her to that rafter and…well, everything that happened after that. Besides, if she was being absolutely fair, they hadn't actually taken any unilateral decisions. All they'd tried to do was keep her safe and, unlike Copeland, hadn't hidden anything from her.

As far as she knew.

"Don't you *ever* think about anything else?" she asked Axel, biting her lower lip to suppress a smile.

"I do my humble best." But Axel looked anything but humble. Her looked more like a golden Greek God and stole a little more of Maddie's breath away each time she looked at him. "My problem is that you blew my mind earlier, babe, and that'll take some forgetting. Still, if you don't want me to think about it, I suppose I could—"

"I know what you're doing. I'm on to you, Cameron. You're trying to distract me with thoughts of your feeble body."

Axel clutched both of his hands over his heart. "She knows how to wound."

"I'm not playing!" she said.

Maddie bit her lip harder to stop herself from really laughing or, worse yet, drooling. Axel was such a hunk, they both were, and if she allowed herself to think about the way her body had melted beneath Riley's skilled fingers, or the way in which Axel went after what he wanted without neglecting her needs, she'd lose focus and they'd all finish up in bed together. Appealing as that prospect might be, right now she needed to keep her mind on her father's murder.

"What did you mean, we'd discuss my going to the center?" she asked. "There's nothing to discuss. I'm going and that's all there is to it."

"Sure you are," Riley replied, remaining annoyingly calm.

"Then why didn't you say so straight out?" She frowned. "I don't understand."

"The way I see it, anyone looking for guinea pigs ain't gonna feel safe plying his trade with all of us there."

"They don't know who you two are?"

"If the bad guy is based around here, then we have to assume that he does. Especially if he has any connection to Copeland."

"This is a slick operation, Maddie," Axel said, suddenly serious. "And the recruiter has the might of a big drugs company behind him. Money's no object, and hacking into just about anything is possible nowadays."

"If I was the recruiter I'd give this week's gathering a miss, wait for us to leave town, and then get back to business as normal."

"Ah, so we need to give him a reason to show himself." Maddie shook her head. "What reason?"

"The guy knows your dad was on to him, or at least getting close, which is why he's dead. If he also knew the major kept a written record of his findings," Riley said, picking the notebook up and waving it in the air, "he'd be damned keen to find out what's in it."

"Ah, now I see." Maddie grinned. "You told Copeland we'd found Dad's notes but didn't let him see them, so they could be even more incriminating than they actually are. They might even name names."

"Right. If you're agreeable, I'll ask Pearson to spread the word that you'll be there tomorrow night. Your dad had something going on, you've found some documents and need to talk to some people about them."

"Why would I go there with them? Why not straight to Copeland?"

"Because you need to be sure of your facts first," Axel said. "Copeland doesn't believe your dad was murdered and you need to find some proof to the contrary."

Maddie flung her arms around Riley's neck and kissed his lips. "That's inspired! Why did I ever doubt you?"

"Dangerous is what it is," Riley replied, briefly returning her kiss and disengaging her arms. "You need to be aware of that before you go charging in."

She bridled. "You think I've forgotten what happened to Dad?"

"I know you haven't." Riley ran his fingers softly across her shoulders. "But this is the big league, babe. You have to promise me not to ever leave the main room where the action is with any of the guys for any reason. Not even Copeland."

"Especially not Copeland," Axel said, scowling. "I still think his people have something to do with this."

"Of course I won't leave. I'm not completely without a brain."

"Just talk to anyone who comes up to you and see if you get any vibes. They might say something to give themselves away, but I wouldn't bet the farm on it. These guys are cautious. What's more likely to happen is that someone will say they have something to tell you but need to talk in private." Riley fixed her with a stern gaze. "Don't fall for it."

"They aren't just slick and cautious, they're damned ruthless," Axel added. "Never lose sight of that."

"I won't, I promise."

"Okay," Riley said. "I'll call Pearson and ask him to set the rumor mill in motion. I already discussed it with him, and he's awaiting my call. Then I'll call Copeland and let him know it's a go."

"Sounds like a plan," Axel said, stretching his arms above his head and winking at Maddie. "You do that and I'll call out for something to eat. I'm starved. Are we all good with Mexican?"

"Works for me," Maddie said.

* * * *

A short time later Riley watched Maddie tucking into fajitas, laughing and flirting with Axel as he wiped sauce from her chin with a paper napkin. He and Maddie had obviously enjoyed themselves. That was good. Axel was an outrageous flirt but, just like Riley, a total commitment-phobe. That was hardly surprising given that he'd had to be mother and father to his three siblings when he was still just a child himself. Before he was even old enough to vote he'd had enough of domesticity to last him a lifetime.

They'd only been here with Maddie for five minutes, but already Riley could see a big change in his buddy. He was hot for their client and didn't seem to care who knew it. That wasn't like the Axel he knew. *Love 'em and leave 'em* had always been his mantra. Could he have found someone with the fire and passion to change that situation? If so then Riley wished him well.

He'd miss their closeness if it happened, of course, but things would never be quite the same between him and Axel again. Making it a permanent cozy threesome was out of the question. Riley had played that game once before, and the pain when it went wrong—when the person he loved more than life itself was snatched from him and there was fuck all he could do to prevent it from happening—was too searing to be borne twice in one lifetime.

No, sir. Riley had the hots for Maddie, too. It was kinda hard not to feel that way about her given her looks, her feisty determination to right the world's wrongs, her enthusiasm between the sheets, the way she did that cute thing with her lower lip—but once this assignment was over he'd still walk away from her. He felt more than momentary disappointment at the thought, but there was no other way.

Still, on the positive side, the assignment wasn't over yet. Since he'd broken his golden rule and played with a client, he might as well compound the felony.

"How did the two of you get along this afternoon?" he asked.

"Funny you should mention that," Axel replied, grinning across the table at Maddie. "But it just so happens our client here still has a lot to learn."

"I'm ready for my next lesson," she said with a smile that sent the heat level in the room skyrocketing.

Both men choked back laughs.

"Her obedience isn't too bad," Axel said conversationally, "but she lacks patience and needs to learn a lot more about the benefits of pain."

"We don't offer pain killers by way of relief," Riley warned her. "The drugs companies make way too much profit as it is."

Maddie giggled. "I'll take my chances."

"You'll take whatever we decide to give you," Riley said sternly.

"Her main issue is impatience," Axel said. "She just can't wait to get it."

"You noticed that, too, did you?" Riley grinned. "Okay, I have a plan."

"Thought you might."

"Have you had enough to eat, Maddie?" Riley asked.

"Yes thanks, that was great."

"Then clear the table and stack the dishwasher," Riley commanded.

She glanced at him, clearly about to object, took one look at the stern set to his features, and complied without a word. Once she was finished and nothing in the kitchen was out of place, she stood next to them and lowered her head, hands clasped demurely in front of her.

"Told you she was a fast learner," Axel said, chuckling.

"Come with us, Maddie."

Riley stood and led them all into the guest suite on the ground floor, next to Maddie's parents' room. She'd allowed Riley to fuck her in the master bedroom last night but probably wouldn't have done if passion hadn't driven all thoughts of their location clean out of her head. He hoped she didn't regret it. Even if that was the case, he figured she wouldn't want to spend the entire night in there with the pair of them, which was what Riley had in mind for them. The guest room had a king-sized bed and plenty of open space—just what he needed.

Riley closed the drapes and switched on a low lamp that threw out just enough light to create a seductive ambiance. He then joined Axel on the settee at the foot of the bed. Maddie stood in front of them, a question in her eyes, the pulse at the base of her throat beating fast enough to indicate extreme excitement. *Baby, you ain't seen nothing yet!*

"Undress," Riley said curtly.

They watched her, both of them tenting their pants as she stepped out of her clothes without the slightest sign of embarrassment. Riley's cock was throbbing like it had a point to prove and they hadn't even started. He breathed deeply, controlling his desires in the same way he was about to teach Maddie to control hers.

"What do you know about tantric sex?" he asked her.

Chapter Thirteen

"Nothing." Maddie shook her head. "Whatever is it?"

"It's kind of an Eastern form of sexual yoga," Axel replied. "You build energy through breathing techniques and then direct that energy through body positions and mental control."

"I don't know anything about yoga, so perhaps it's not such a good idea."

Riley chuckled. "There's a hell of a lot more to yoga than standing on your head or doing the lotus thing. Like Axel said, it's as much about the power of the mind as that of the body."

"But flexibility does help," Axel said, winking at her. "And I already know you're pretty damned flexible."

"Okay." Maddie was intrigued. "Tell me more."

"We need you to enter an altered state where the three of us merge with each other and the cosmos. If you get it right it's a really diverse orgasmic experience and a great way to learn patience."

"Hmm, patience?" She plucked her lower lip with her forefinger. "Definitely not my strong point."

"Precisely, and that means you're missing out on a hell of a lot," Axel replied.

"I've heard tantric sex described as energy working its way up and down the spine and then extending from the body through the head and hovering over it like a cobra," Riley said, fixing her with a gaze that promised to deliver.

Maddie canted her head and smiled at them. "Well, that sounds amazing. Do you think I can do it?"

"You can do anything you set your mind to," Axel said. "This is all about focusing the power of the mind, remember. Tantra, done right, gives orgasms that are indescribable in their intensity."

Riley grabbed a large beanbag from the corner of the room and set it on the floor, against the wall.

"Sit down on that, cross your legs, and close your eyes," he said.

Maddie did as he asked.

"Good girl. Now breathe real slow and deep. Think about your breathing. Really concentrate on it." Riley paused, presumably giving her a moment to comply. "Empty your mind of absolutely everything and relax. Relax through your shoulders, your arms, your belly, your legs…that's right, let yourself drift. Breathing deeply and trusting yourself to your partners' care is the key. This is all about trust, Maddie. We need to get you into the zone, the space if you like, where your body and mind are separated."

"We need you to channel all the sexual energy that would normally leave you during orgasm back into your body," Axel said in a low, hypnotic tone. "It prolongs the act and increases potent sexual energy. If your objective is solely to orgasm you miss the amazing range of feelings that act as a prelude to good sex. Riley was right. This is the perfect way to teach you patience."

"We need candles, soft music, oils, and all that stuff to do this right," Riley said. "But we don't have those things, so we're just gonna have to make do."

Maddie, still with her eyes closed, nodded. She felt strangely relaxed but wasn't too sure about all this *delaying the moment* business. Far as she was concerned, the moment couldn't come soon enough. They still had a lot of work to do if they expected her to become a convert.

"Think of the ocean lapping against a sandy shore on a warm day," Axel said in a soft, lazy voice. "Feel the sun burning into your skin, feel your nipples tingling because you forgot to put on your swimsuit. A bunch of men are looking at you because you're on a public beach with no clothes on. You don't mind. They're strangers, but you want to embrace them. You love the world, you're sensually receptive to the guys watching you because they make you feel so fucking horny and you want the whole damned universe to feel as good as you do right now."

"Hmm." Maddie rotated her shoulders and let out a long breath.

"Open your eyes, darlin', and look at us," Riley said softly.

She did so and found them both standing in front of her, legs slightly apart, bulges jutting against their zippers. In unison they pulled their T-shirts over their heads and threw them aside. Maddie simply stared, aware that her eyes were probably bulging. Not that she gave a shit. It wasn't every day a girl got to feast her eyes on two such lean, hard torsos, muscles rippling, not an ounce of fat to spoil the view. Two for the price of one, as well. Maddie didn't know what she'd done to get herself in this position, but she intended to enjoy every second.

They reached for their zippers, lowered their pants, and stepped out of them, along with their underwear. Now they were as naked as she was. Their cocks were enormous, thick, hard, and twitching. They must be as desperate as she was, but it didn't seem to bother them. Presumably they practiced what they preached and knew how to control their needs. Damn it, she didn't want them to be in control. She wanted them to be wild. To grab hold of her, to be brutal in taking what they needed, to...Hell, this was pure torture!

"We're going to harmonize our breathing, Maddie," Riley said, fixing her with a seductive look.

"We're going to *what!*"

"Straighten your legs out." Riley straddled her lap as he spoke but took his weight on his knees. "This is the yab-yom position. I'm going to put my mouth up real close to yours. When you breathe out, I'll draw your breath in, and vice versa. As you exhale, consciously try to energize the breath. Can you do that for me?"

Is he serious? "I guess I can try, but I have to tell you—"

"Shush!"

"Keep your eyes open, Maddie," Axel said. "Seeing your partner's reactions is one of the fundamentals of deep, intimate connection. Truly witnessing the act of love is profoundly transformative."

She wanted to shout that Riley didn't love her—neither of them did—but already felt an odd transformation taking place inside her as they shared one another's air. She didn't want to spoil the moment by correcting Axel's slip of the tongue, but really, Riley and Axel were two of the most contained men she'd ever met. She suspected they didn't usually do this sort of stuff with their clients but didn't read too much into that. Besides, they weren't the only ones carrying emotional baggage that precluded commitment. This was just fun. She didn't care that they felt nothing for her.

She absolutely didn't!

"You feel any changes yet?" Axel asked her.

"Hmm yes, I feel kinda like I'm out of my body." She frowned. "Is that weird?"

"Nope." Axel sounded smug. "It's precisely what you're supposed to feel. Experts at this stuff commonly have orgasms that last for more than twenty minutes."

"You're kidding me!"

Axel chuckled. "Worth working toward, don't you think?"

Maddie couldn't believe the intensity of the tingling sensations already passing through her body. Her nipples hardened, a deeply disturbing thrill jolted her gut and, of course, liquid poured from her pussy. She was in a state of totally sensual awareness, yet neither one of them had laid so much as a finger on her. It was surreal.

The breathing thing seemed to go on for ages. All impatience had now left Maddie, and she would have been content to remain right where she was, sharing the same air as the hunk-with-a-hard-on who was straddling her body, forever. Presumably she'd reached *the zone* they'd been telling her about because Riley finally moved and Maddie couldn't help it when a small moan of protest slipped past her lips.

"Don't worry, sugar," Axel said, chuckling. "Riley ain't done with you yet."

She wanted to say she was glad to hear it but remembered just in time that she wasn't supposed to speak unless asked a question.

"The fusion position is a favorite in Kama Sutra," Riley said. "Done right you'll have a tantric G-spot orgasm that'll blow your entire body."

A G-spot orgasm? Maddie tried to not to feel disappointed. She could give herself one of those. Maddie wouldn't admit it because she didn't want to get into a discussion about her sexual history, but self-induced orgasms were about the only action she'd seen for a long time before meeting these guys, and she was hoping for a damned sight better than that from them today.

"Position yourself over me, darlin'," Riley said. "Keep breathing the same way, slow and deep, stay in the zone, and keep your eyes open."

Riley helped her to lower herself so that her legs rested beside his chest. Sitting up, he placed his arms behind his torso and leaned his weight on them.

"Lean back and rest your arms between my legs," he said.

"Condom," Riley said to Axel.

"Don't unless you want to," Maddie said. "I have birth control covered and I'm clean."

"You sure?"

"Absolutely."

Riley finally touched her, but only briefly so he could part her slick folds and slide his glorious cock into her. She shivered as he filled her completely and instinctively closed her eyes to absorb the moment.

"Eyes open!" Axel, who appeared to have adopted the role of referee, tapped her thigh and Maddie's eyes flew open again.

"Use your arms and legs to rock yourself on my cock, darlin'," Riley said, fixing her with a deeply sensual gaze. "It has to be an in-and-out motion, a bit like a piston. The angle and the seductive position make it highly erotic."

"Like this?"

"Exactly like that, honey. Work it as deep as you need it. That's right." Riley smiled at her. "Now you've got it. You feel the heat?"

"Yes, I feel it."

She moaned softly but Riley remained passive, leaving her to take what she needed without giving her any help.

"Keep breathing slowly, sweet thing, and let it build in its own time."

At last she was free to set the pace, which would be fast and frantic. Get it done. Get it over with before he hurts you. Except this man would never do anything to hurt her. Maddie's brief panic attack subsided and she concentrated on the way she felt, pinioned by Riley's massive cock that stretched her to full capacity. She could ride it like she was the star act at a rodeo if she wanted to because she was the one in charge.

To her astonishment she had no wish to rush and worked slowly to increase the friction, her perceptions heighted by all the stuff that had gone before. Perhaps there was something to this tantric business after all. With her eyes open she could see how hard Riley was straining to hold back. That knowledge empowered her, filling her with the desire to keep him waiting so long that his self-restraint burst. She glanced sideways, saw how aroused Axel was, and it was her undoing. He noticed her looking, winked as he fisted his own cock, and her newfound willpower disappeared into the ether.

The most amazing cocktail of desire and heady passion ran riot through her insides. Exquisite shards of the most intense sensation spiraled out from her gut to reach the extremities of her limbs before homing in on her sweet spot. She moved faster, aware this was nothing like the stuff she did on her own.

"Ohmygod! Riley, this is amazing!"

She closed around him and shattered, screaming his name as she came, and then came some more. Riley held firm, and she rode his cock for what seemed like minutes. Could it really have been that long? It was certainly longer and far more intense than anything she'd known before.

"How did that happen?" she asked, opening her eyes and shaking her head. "I've never known anything like it."

"We did warn you," Axel replied, looking smug.

"Come on, babe."

Riley withdrew, helped her to her feet, and the three of them deposited themselves on the bed.

"You like tantric?" Riley asked, grinning.

"I think I could get addicted. My body's still humming." She glanced at Riley, whose cock was still rigidly erect. "But you didn't—"

"That was for you."

"Now it's our turn," Axel added, grinning at her.

* * * *

Riley lay flat on his back, giving himself a moment to recover. It took a damned sight longer to recover from *not* coming, he knew from experience. Still, it had been worth it just to see the look of total astonishment on Maddie's face when she reaped the benefits of holding back. He prided himself on his self-control, but how he'd not lost it then and there when he felt her closing about him he'd never know. She was something else, and if things were different...Shit, things were the way they were.

Get over yourself, buddy.

Axel would take over now. They didn't need to discuss it. It was just how they operated.

"Your body's got a lot more humming to do yet," Axel said. "Get on your hands and knees for me, honey."

As soon as Maddie had done so Riley tossed Axel a tube of lube and he applied a liberal amount to her ass, smoothing it carefully into the crack between her cheeks and rimming her anus with a slick finger.

"We need to get you thinking about anal sex," he said.

"I'm willing to give it a go."

"I know you are," Riley said, laughing. "You're so hot for us right now that you'd do just about anything we asked."

"Yes," she said breathlessly. "You've broadened my horizons, and I want you both."

"And you'll get us, but first you need to have that cute ass spanked, which just happens to be Axel's specialty."

Riley threw Axel a plastic spatula he'd found in a kitchen drawer. Axel flexed it against his hand, rested it against her butt, then lifted it and brought it down lightly. The sound of it making contact with her flesh was loud in the otherwise-quiet room. Maddie flinched but held her position.

"Wait for the tingling to warm your insides," Riley said softly. "Just remember that breathing technique and it'll work better."

"It'll work better still, the harder I spank you," Axel assured her.

A man of his word, Axel repeated the procedure but put more strength behind it this time. Maddie cried out, but Riley didn't think she was in any discomfort.

"Remember the safety word," Axel said. "If it gets too much, we'll stop at once."

"I don't want you to stop," she said breathlessly. "Everything we've done so far has been new, and it feels liberating."

Laughing, Riley slid beneath her, sideways on, so that his erection was directly beneath her sweet lips.

"Suck it, darlin'," he said gruffly.

Her lips closed around him, sending Riley directly to his version of heaven. His thick cock filled to danger level when she licked him from its tip right down to his balls and then back again. Riley sucked in a breath. Shit, she was a little too good at this. The sound of Axel spanking her echoed round the room, as did the elevation in Maddie's breathing. If Axel was acting true to form he'd have slid a couple of fingers into her backside and got her used to the feeling. Shame they didn't have a butt plug with them, but that was a situation that could soon be rectified. When, no if, they played with Maddie as a threesome again then Riley would have a few tools of the trade with him.

"You okay, darlin'?" Axel asked. "I know you can't speak with your mouthful but I'm guessing you're good with this."

She almost bit Riley's cock in two, presumably because Axel was rubbing her clit with his thumb at the same time as he spanked her.

"Relax, honey," he said. "We do this my way or not at all."

Somehow she managed to emit a moan, even though her mouth was full to capacity. She was sucking Riley now like she had a point to prove. He closed his eyes, practicing what he'd just preached to Maddie and breathing slow and deep, delaying the moment, or so he hoped. But there were some things that just plain refused to be delayed. The seductive feel of Maddie's tongue lathing his cock, the way her lips pushed back his foreskin and tickled his sensitive head, was more than any man could possible withstand. He growled at her, grabbed the back of her neck, and forced her head down until he was buried deep at the back of her throat. Then he let it all go, spurting an endless stream of sperm that she gamely swallowed as fast as she could.

Riley pulled out of her mouth, lay with his hands behind his head, and watched the show. Axel had slid into Maddie's tight pussy from behind and was fucking her hard. And she was loving it, pushing back against him, taking him as deep as he could get. Riley watched her face as a kaleidoscope of emotions flitted across it. The way her tits swung beneath her as Axel plundered her body was enough to get Riley erect again. Shit, what was she doing to him?

He'd give a lot to know why she was so comparatively naïve when it came to sex. He'd go so far as to say she'd almost been afraid of it before they took her in hand. What was it she wasn't telling them? Riley returned his attention to the show Maddie and Axel were putting on, completely into one another, and reminded himself it was none of his damned business what Maddie was holding back from them. One way or another, the matter with Maddie's dad's death would be cleared up within the next couple of days and he and Axel would be out of here.

"That feels so fucking good!" Maddie cried as her body went into a series of wild spasms. "Keep doing it, Axel. I can't stop coming."

"I'm with you there, babe," Axel grunted.

Riley watched as Axel screwed his eyes tight and clearly gave her everything he had.

Chapter Fourteen

The first thing that occurred to Maddie when she opened her eyes the following morning was that she wasn't in her own bed. Nor was she alone. Instead she was squashed between two large, warm bodies. Her head was resting not on a pillow but on a solid chest that was a little too comfortable. A heavy arm rested across her belly from the opposite side. She jerked upright... What the devil?

"What's wrong, babe?"

The sound of Riley's voice calmed her, as did the familiar sight of the guest suite.

"I forgot, just for a minute."

Axel sat up on her other side, his blond curls sticking up at odd angels and making him appear like an endearing little boy.

"It's okay," he said, swooping in for a kiss. "I guess we take some getting used to."

Reassured, Maddie lay flat on her back again, noticing things about herself that hadn't been immediately apparent when she awoke. Like her lips felt twice their usual size, her body was pleasantly sore and her mind felt lighter than it had for weeks. Had they really done all that stuff last night, right down to playing *catch me if you can* in the shower, or was it her imagination? She glanced from one of them to the other and knew she hadn't imagined anything. She simply didn't have it in her to make that sort of stuff up. They really had made her body sing like a diva.

Incredible!

"Hmm, sleepy," she said, nestling her head on Axel's shoulder for a change.

"How sleepy?" Riley asked, his handsome face looming over hers, a challenge lighting his eyes.

"Well, now you come to mention it, not *that* sleepy," she replied, aware of a massive erection pressing into her thigh.

"That's good," Axel said, "because we have a unique way of starting our days whenever we get the chance."

"This I must hear."

Riley's throaty chuckle was wickedly suggestive. "We're men of action, darlin', not words."

And then they were on her—both of them at the same time, hands and teeth everywhere. Rough and gentle. Hard and soft. Completely and totally dominant. And she loved every second of it. Her nipples were tweaked and bitten, erogenous zones she was unaware she possessed tortured until she begged for mercy. A strong pair of hands pushed her onto her side, and this time it was Riley who applied something cool to her backside. Axel flipped himself upside down and feasted on her clit, his mobile tongue checking out every inch of pussy until she thought she might very well die from anticipation. She was so taken up with what he was doing that she was only vaguely conscious of Riley's fingers exploring her anus.

"Don't tense up on me, babe," he said, his warm breath peppering her shoulder as he whispered the words into her ear, as smooth and reassuring as a used-car salesman. "This'll blow your mind, if you'll just relax and trust me. Remember the breathing technique."

How could she ever forget? Axel was bringing her closer and closer to orgasm. His entire face was buried in her mound, his tongue delivering long, vigorous licks and then deft persistent flicks that drove her increasingly wild. On the point of release, her entire body tensed when she sensed the tip of Riley's cock invading her anus.

"Let me in, darlin'," he said on a crooning voice. "You'll be glad you did, I promise you."

That appeared to be Axel's cue to increase the pressure he was putting on her pussy. She dug the fingers of one hand into his curls, recalled the breathing thing, and felt the tension drain from her body.

"Good girl!"

Riley slipped a little deeper. The burning sensation she'd felt gave way to the most overwhelmingly sensual tingling she'd ever known.

"Oh!" she said, for once lost for words. "That's...well, that's, er—"

"Let's take this slow and easy, darlin'," Riley said softly." I don't want to hurt you."

Maddie realized she was supposed to keep still, but it was asking too much. She had one hunk feeding on her cunt and another sliding his huge cock into her ass. She was on fire, desperate need flowing through her like molten lead, and she was unable to prevent herself from moving her pelvis as she absorbed all that was on offer. She expected to be chastised, but instead they acted like a well-oiled machine, seeming to know exactly how long to torture her before having mercy and letting her come.

No sooner had Axel brought her to orgasm than the reality of what Riley was doing to her hit home. His huge cock filled her, and the spurt of panic she'd felt turned to desire. This was like nothing she'd ever known before, the sensation indescribable. Wanton carnality ripped through her bloodstream as Riley carefully worked her ass. The sensation burned and intensified as her body when into spasm. All hell was let loose inside her before the aftershock of the orgasm Axel had given her even had a chance to fade. One climax segued into a second, less violent but far deeper feeling of satiation.

"Wow!" was all she managed to say as Riley slipped out of her and Maddie rolled onto her back, totally boneless.

"Our pleasure," Axel said, kissing her, her own juices still slick on his lips. "And just so you know, you taste devastatingly erotic. Sweeter than vintage wine, as it happens."

"Does eroticism have a taste?"

"Yeah," they said in unison. "It tastes like you."

She protested when one of them lifted her from the bed and took her to the shower. She absolutely didn't want to move because it would spoil the moment. She needed to store away in her memory everything they'd done to her so she could relive the experiences vicariously once they'd gone. Only when the three of them had crowded into the stall and Riley started soaping her body did it occur to her that Axel hadn't had his share of the fun.

"Be my guest," he said, when she mentioned it.

Laughing, she slid to her knees beneath the hot jets of water and allowed them to cascade over her head as she took him into her mouth.

* * * *

After their shower Riley and Axel left Maddie sleeping again. Both men knew without having to ask that she'd never been through a sexathon like the one she'd just experienced, and she'd need some recovery time.

"Best damned way I can think of to distract her from what she has to do this evening," Riley said, setting the coffee maker working.

Axel shook his head. "She's damned hot is all I know."

"Yeah, yeah."

Axel shot his buddy a look. "I was only sayin'. And she'd make a great sub. We need to give her some more training, but it won't take much. She's a natural."

"No time," Riley said curtly. "We'll be out of here in a day or two."

Axel leaned across the counter and got his face close up to Riley's. "What are you afraid of?"

"Nothing." Riley looked away. "She's different, I'll give you that. If she wasn't then this wouldn't be happing, but for me it's as far as it goes. But, hey, if you want to—"

"You know I don't."

"Well then."

"Even if I did want, she has a life in New York, friends, boyfriends…stuff."

Axel shrugged, but Riley knew him too well to be deceived. He was tempted, sorely tempted to break his self-imposed commitment embargo. Riley could understand that. If he could just shake images of Stella, her suffering, what they both went through during the course of her illness, then just maybe he'd feel the same way. Problem was, he'd never been able to forget all that pain. No, it was safer to keep his head and heart separate when it came to women.

"Probably." Riley extracted the ingredients for a big fry-up from the fridge. "Anyway, we need to concentrate on arrangements for this evening."

"Right, yeah, of course we do."

They chatted it through as they ate, trying to anticipate every possible hitch.

"Just so long as she remembers never to leave the room with anyone, we'll be okay," Riley said, stretching his arms about his head and yawning. "There's nothing else we can do between now and then, so we might as well relax."

Riley's phone rang several times. Copeland checking that everything was still on. Pearson to say he'd spread the word. The regulars were glad Maddie would be coming along, but no one seemed especially interested.

Riley called Raoul and told him what the plan was.

"Don't see how else you can play it," Raoul replied. "But I don't like the idea of Maddie being in the direct line of fire."

"We're not ecstatic about it ourselves, but we can't think of any other way."

"Yeah, I hear you. Just keep that gal safe."

"Count on it," Riley replied before cutting the connection.

Maddie appeared shortly after that, looking deliciously rumpled and thoroughly satiated. Riley insisted on cooking her breakfast and then sat down next to her to make sure she ate it all.

"Sex obviously gives her an appetite as well." Axel laughed as he cleared her plate. "It makes us starving."

"Everything makes you two starving," Maddie replied, rolling her eyes.

"Yeah well, there is that."

"Our antics have reacquainted me with a few muscles I'd forgotten about," Maddie said, grimacing when she moved.

"Go on, babe," Axel chided. "Admit it. It was worth every ache and pain."

She did another eye roll. "Your modesty could use some work."

It was near lunchtime when Maddie finished her breakfast. Riley figured that was a good thing because there was now less time to get through before heading off to the center. Which also meant there was less time for her to get nervous. He could think of a lot of inventive ways to fill the time in between but reined in his imagination and offered his and Axel's help with sorting out her father's study.

"There won't be anything to help with our inquiry in there," he said. "Your dad was far too canny for that. But still, it all has to be gone through, and three pairs of hands are better than one."

"Sure, thanks," she said. "Let's make a start."

"You two go ahead. I just need to pop into town real quick," Riley said. "I have an errand to run, but I'll be right back."

"Anything to get out of doing the real work," Axel quipped.

Riley shot him the finger, grabbed the keys to their truck, and disappeared out the door. He found the store he needed, bought up half of it, and returned to do his share of the work.

They spent the next two hours making inroads into the hundreds of files Maddie's father had accumulated, only speaking when they needed to ask her what to do with stuff.

The methodical work appeared to calm her, and when Riley called a halt, suggesting there was just time for a sandwich before they headed off, she seemed surprised that so much time had passed.

Axel was on sandwich duty, and when they'd eaten all they could, Maddie excused herself to go and change. Her room was upstairs, but the guys heard her rummaging about in her parents' room.

"What's that all about?" Axel asked.

Riley shrugged. "I guess we'll find out soon enough."

Maddie returned a short time later in clean jeans, a loose long-sleeved top, and a light jacket. Around her neck was a long strand of unusual crystal beads. Riley commented on it.

"It was a favorite of my mom's," she replied. "It belonged to her mother and her mother before her. Its only value is sentimental, and Dad often suggested I ought to take it but I couldn't...well, I couldn't bring myself to touch any of her stuff."

"That's understandable," Riley said.

"But thanks to you two I've managed to get over that." She lifted her shoulders. "I know it's stupid, but wearing Mom's beads tonight will be like a talisman. A good-luck charm."

"Not in the least bit silly," Axel said, blowing her a kiss. "Whatever works for you."

The guys stuck to their normal uniform of jeans, T-shirts, and leather jackets. Both had sidearms in holsters beneath their jackets.

"All set?" Riley asked her.

"As I'll ever be."

"You can still change your mind."

"Yeah, but that's not gonna happen. Come on, let's take your truck."

Traffic was light and they got to the center early. John Reynolds greeted them when they walked in. The place was busier than when Riley had last visited, but he could see over Reynolds's shoulder that the main room was still thin on bodies.

"Nice to see you again," Reynolds said. "Some of the men will enjoy talking to you. Hope you're prepared to chew the fat."

"Of course." Riley shook his hand and then introduced Axel and Maddie.

"Ms. McGuire, allow me to say how much I enjoyed your father's company." He shook his head. "Such a tragedy."

"Thank you, Mr. Reynolds. That means a lot."

"Why don't you go on through and mingle? It's early yet, but the place will fill up before long. Free food and the company of other service personnel are hard for even the most antisocial vet to resist."

"We'll do that."

As soon as they reached the threshold, Riley and Axel held back and Maddie walked into the melee alone. Anyone watching them would know they were together, but the point was to make Maddie accessible. Riley glanced around and saw Copeland already there, along with his female sidekick, Shirley Mance. Pearson was there, too, but only acknowledged Riley with the slightest inclination of his head.

"Here we go," Riley said, grabbing a beer and taking a swig. "Bring it on!"

* * * *

Maddie was a mixture of self-doubt and determination as she plunged into that room. There were a few other women there, but they were outnumbered ten to one by an abundance of testosterone. She attracted a lot of attention, but no one tried to make a move on her. She recognized a couple of old friends of her father's and fell into conversation with them. This business had made her suspicious of everyone, including them. It had made her doubt everything she'd once taken for granted, and she was so on edge that she found it hard to behave naturally.

She understood now what Riley and Axel had done for her. She hadn't realized she was nervous about doing this, but they obviously had, and she had to say, their methods of distraction had a lot going for them. She squeezed her legs together to prevent the inevitable flow of liquid that she'd grown to expect whenever she thought about their sexploits, and concentrated on what a retired captain was saying to her.

An ever-changing sea of people swirled around Maddie as the room filled and the noise level increased. Several times she lost sight of Riley and Axel but took comfort from the fact that they had to be keeping her in their sights. So, too, did Copeland and the rest of his people. Not that it was necessary because so far nothing out of the ordinary had occurred. Riley must have been right. Whoever was behind this wouldn't risk coming down here today—not with Riley and Axel watching her back. It had been a massive waste of time. Even so, she couldn't seem to shake the trickling premonition that had gripped her the moment she walked into this place.

Sticking to soda, Maddie helped herself to another glass and to a plateful of food, just for something to do. She felt Riley's gaze boring into her back but didn't acknowledge him. Instead she fell into conversation with a guy who'd just introduced himself. He seemed keen to keep her to himself, and for the first time Maddie wondered if she'd finally hit pay dirt.

Ten minutes later she'd almost lost the will to live when the man had told her, in excruciating detail, exactly what was wrong with the youth of today.

"Excuse me for a moment please."

Maddie desperately needed to find the restroom. Recalling the promise she'd made to Riley never to leave the room alone, she sought out Shirley Mance.

"Not that I need my hand held or anything," she said apologetically.

"No problem." Shirley put her glass down. "I could do with the bathroom myself."

Maddie glanced over her shoulder at Riley. She tilted her head in the direction of the bathrooms, and he nodded as though giving her permission.

"I can imagine worse jailors," Shirley said, observing the exchange and grinning.

Maddie laughed. "There is that, I suppose."

"Come on, it's this way."

They walked into a very small restroom, which was meticulously clean.

"Not many women in this place," Shirley explained. "So the lion's share of the facilities are reserved for the men."

"That seems fair."

There was just one toilet cubicle, a shower and a wash basin. Shirley shot the bolt across the outer door.

"I don't think anyone will...Hey, what the hell do you think you're doing?"

Maddie had placed her purse on the vanity. Shirley picked it up and tipped the contents into the basin, which was when realization came crashing in on Maddie.

"It's you," she said, clapping a hand over her mouth. "You're the creep who's conning the vets."

Chapter Fifteen

"They've been in there for a hell of a long time," Axel said, scowling.

Riley shrugged. "You know what women are like."

"Yes, but I didn't think Maddie was into all that primping and sharing-secrets stuff, especially with a woman she barely knows."

"Looks like this is a bust," Riley said, yawning. "Maddie hasn't given any indication that anyone who's spoken to her is the slightest bit suspicious, and I haven't sensed anything's wrong. Still, we'll give it another half hour."

"Shame, I thought it would work." Axel grinned. "Does that give us an excuse to stay a bit longer with the lovely Maddie?"

"I already told you, buddy. You don't need to invent excuses."

The two men had subconsciously wandered toward the corridor leading to the bathrooms. There was a line forming outside the ladies' room, and mutterings about the length of time its occupants were taking. Pearson happened to pass them at that moment and Riley grabbed his arm, his danger antennae now on high alert.

"How many toilets in there?" he asked tersely.

"Just the one."

Riley and Axel barged through the crowd and tried the door to the ladies' bathroom. It was locked. Riley hammered on it with his fist.

"Are you okay, Maddie?" he yelled.

No answer.

"Is there a back way out of there?" he asked Pearson.

"No, just a window."

"Fuck! Stand back."

Quite a crowd had now gathered as Riley and Axel put their shoulders to the door and shoved as hard as they could. The lock popped and they fell into the room. Maddie's purse was upended in the basin, but there was no sign of her. The window was banging open.

"Shit!" Riley and Axel said together.

"What's happened?" Copeland asked, running in to join them.

"Your captain," Riley replied. "How well do you know her?"

"It's her?" Copeland looked genuinely shocked. "But she's worked with me for a long time, and I trusted her completely. I had absolutely no idea."

"You told her Maddie was bringing the papers here tonight?"

"Well yes, she needed to know."

"Come on, we have to find them."

Riley and Axel ran back down the corridor, Copeland at their heels. Riley tried to remember the external layout of the place and figured the bathroom window probably gave out onto the narrow road leading to the parking garage.

"She has to be desperate to do something so public, especially when she knew it was a trap," Riley said as he raced along.

"She *is* desperate," Axel replied. "If she thought she'd been named then she had no choice but to try and get those papers. She knew Maddie would need to use the restroom sooner or later and would ask her to go with her."

"Shit, we played right into her slimy hands," Riley said grimly. "Her cover's blown now, which means she has nothing to lose. That makes her dangerous."

"Where would she have gone?" Axel asked Copeland as they stood outside the bathroom window, looking up and down the street. There was no sign of either Maddie or Mance. That would have been too easy.

"Give me a moment to think."

"There's no time," Riley replied, resisting the urge to shake the man. "Maddie's life's on the line here."

"Presumably Mance was the middle-woman for whoever's doing this," Axel said.

"Yeah, so someone would have been waiting, probably with a car, for them to come through this window. Maddie wouldn't have gone willingly."

"Unless Mance pulled a gun on her."

Riley swore. "I still think someone had to be waiting out here for them."

"They couldn't have parked here. The street's too narrow."

"That's true." Riley nodded. "The accomplice would have no idea when they'd come through the window—"

"Unless Mance rang his cell."

"Even so, a car blocking the road this narrow for even a short time would have been noticed."

"So you think she was dragged off to a car nearby."

"Did Mance drive herself here?"

"No," Copeland replied. "She came with me. There's a strip mall just around the corner. If she has an accomplice, I'm betting he's parked up there."

"Why not the parking garage?" Riley asked.

"Quicker to get away from a mall that's not under cover."

"Okay, show me."

They ran off in that direction, but there was nothing in the mall's parking lot to attract their attention.

"They couldn't have gotten away so quickly," Riley said. "We're only a minute or two behind them, I'm sure, and Maddie would have dragged her feet. They must have gone the other way."

"The other direction just leads to a block of condos," Copeland said.

"We need to check it out. It's all we have to go on."

Riley ran back so fast that he almost missed it.

"Hold up!" he yelled, stopping abruptly.

"What is it?" Axel asked.

Riley was sick with worry for Maddie. Even so, he couldn't prevent a small admiring smile from breaking through his defenses.

"This," he said, holding up a crystal bead. "Our girl has left us a trail."

* * * *

At first Maddie was too angry to be afraid. How could she have been so dense? She'd liked Shirley Mance on the several occasions they'd met, wishing she could have dealt with her rather than that stuffed shirt Copeland. What did that say about her ability to read people?

"How could you do it?" she asked as they glared at one another across the small bathroom. "Those men have given their all for this country and you exploit them like their lives are worth nothing."

"Where're your father's notes?"

"Somewhere you'll never find them."

"You'd better hope for your sake that I do. You're no use to me without them."

"And I'll be surplus to requirements if I hand them over, so why would I do that?"

"I'm no killer."

"Really?" Maddie sent her a quelling glance. "Tell that to the guys who disappeared."

"I was done here anyway. Your dear dad stirred things up and got Copeland involved, so it was getting too risky. Besides, I've made enough out of it and I just need time to get away. It's all arranged, but I can't do that until I'm sure the people I work for are safe."

"Of course you can't," Maddie said sarcastically.

"Tell me what names are in those notes."

"No."

"Oh, for God's sake! I don't have time for this." Mance extracted her cell phone from her pocket and hit the dial button. "We're coming out," she said to the person who answered.

"I'm not going anywhere," Maddie said, folding her arms across her chest.

"Oh yes you are."

Mance drew a pistol from her purse and nodded toward the window. "I *will* use this gun if I have to," she said. "Never doubt it."

"With a roomful of ex-soldiers on the other side of that door?" Maddie quirked a brow. "I don't think so."

"And I don't think you realize what you're dealing with. I'm just a very small cog in a huge wheel. And, just like you, I'm expendable if I don't clear up this mess. So, you see, I have nothing to lose." She jerked the gun toward the window. "Open it!"

Maddie saw the stark determination in Mance's eye and knew she meant what she said. She would use the gun because she was more afraid of the people she worked for than of what would happen to her if she was caught.

Maddie thought fast. Riley and Axel would soon miss her. She just needed to play for time. As slowly as she thought she could get away with, she reached up for the window catch, pretending not to be able to reach it.

"Go on, you can do it."

"It's stuck."

Mance swore, walked up behind Maddie, jammed the barrel of the gun into her kidneys, and reached for the catch herself. It opened easily.

"Climb through."

This was all happening too fast. Maddie needed to do something to slow the process down. She thought about yelling for help, but the restroom was too remote for her to be heard. With no other choice available to her she closed the toilet lid, clambered up onto it, and pulled herself through the open window frame. Perhaps she could drop down on the outside and run for it.

She abandoned that idea when she saw a bull of a man standing directly outside, waiting to catch her. Mance followed quickly behind her. The man took one of Maddie's arms, Mance took the other, and her feet barely touched the ground as they sped her away. Anger gave way to fear, but along with that fear came the determination to survive. She had a lot more to learn from Riley and Axel yet. *Hold that thought!*

Struggling against the man's iron grip, Maddie's fingers got caught in her strand of crystals and an idea occurred to her. The man and Mance seemed intent upon spiriting her away and were looking straight ahead, not at her. Trying not to use anything other than her fingers because sudden jolting of her arms might alert them, Maddie took three attempts to break the strand of crystals and caught the first few as they trickled into her hands.

Then she allowed them to drop onto the ground, one precious bead at a time, like an untidy snail's trail.

Maddie was frog-marched into an apartment block, up two flights of cracked concrete stairs to the second floor. An open walkway with an iron railing ran along the outside of the individual doors. Mance stopped outside of number 207 and the man released her arm in order to unlock the door. Maddie managed to drop her final crystal just before she was shoved through the door. She heard it bounce and then roll toward the iron railing. *Please God don't let it fall over the edge.* If it did, Riley and Axel would never find her.

* * * *

The trail of crystals was spasmodic but sufficient for the guys to realize Maddie was being taken to the nearest apartment block. It was an old building overdue for renovation. Cheap rents for transient residents, Riley assumed. It was that sort of district. Copeland had his men deployed around the area. No one was getting out, that was for sure. Riley didn't give a fuck about Mance and her co-conspirators. His only priority was getting Maddie out in one piece. *Then* he'd go after the bad guys and they'd regret the fucking day they were born. He seldom allowed his temper to get the better of him in combat situations, but the manner in which these cowards had murdered Maddie's father and appeared to have the same fate in mind for her made for an exception to the rule. He only hoped she'd had the presence of mind to pretend that *he* had the papers. That would be enough to keep her alive until Riley and Axel could rescue her.

"They used the stairs," Axel said, pointing to a crystal halfway up the first flight.

"If they've got her inside an apartment then we're fucked," Copeland said. "If we break in, they'll shoot her."

"Let's find the apartment first," Riley said. "Then we'll think up a plan."

The three of them ran lightly up two flights and along the landing on the second floor. There was one crystal at the beginning of the walkway, and then nothing.

"Shit!" Riley thumped his fist against the nearest wall. "We have no idea which apartment they're in."

It wasn't the sort of block that had a concierge, so they didn't have a clue what to do next. Knocking on doors could get Maddie killed.

"We need to keep looking," Axel said. "Unless she ran out of crystals, there must be another one somewhere."

All three men crouched along the landing, not wishing to be seen from any of the apartments.

Nothing.

"Look in here," Riley said, pointing to the gutter that ran along the edge of the walkway. "It might have rolled off."

It was Copeland who found it. He called quietly to the others, who joined him at the middle of the walkway.

"Only problem is, which apartment?" Axel asked. "It's fallen midway between two doors, and both of them have got the drapes closed."

Riley motioned to the others to join him at the end of the walkway, in an alcove close to the elevators.

"The way I see it," he said, "they've improvised. I'm guessing this is a place where they kept vets before moving them on, and they're using it today to hold Maddie until they get the papers. Mance won't want the people she works for to know that she fucked up and we're onto her, so she'll try and clean up her own mess."

"Which means," Axel added, "that it's probably just her and one other guy in there."

"Right. She would have needed some local guy to look after the vets until they were moved on."

"Still, it only takes one person with a gun, and there has to be at least two of them."

"Let's see if we can reduce the odds. You got Mance's number in your cell?" he asked Copeland.

"You're assuming an awful lot," Copeland said.

"It's a case of best guessing," Riley replied tersely. "Besides, have you got a better idea?"

"No, and of course I have her number."

He handed his phone to Riley, who hit the dial button. Mance answered on the first ring.

"It's Maddox," he said. "I have what you want."

"Be outside the center in five minutes. If it checks out, you get her back."

"How do I know you'll let her go?"

"Because I'm in this for money and I don't do murder."

Riley made a lot of tutting noises. "Let me talk to her, or it's no dice."

"Just a moment."

"Riley?" Maddie sounded as mad as hell.

"You okay?" he asked.

"Two of them to kidnap little ol' me."

Mance's voice came back on the phone, but Riley already had his suspicions confirmed. Got to hand it to Maddie, she was smart.

"All right, I guess I have no choice. I'll see you in five."

"Not me. My associate will find you."

The line went dead.

"Now we wait," Riley said.

Less than a minute later heavy footsteps echoed along the walkway. Riley and Axel brought the guy down before he even realized they were there. They took his handgun and pushed him none too gently against the wall. Riley was disappointed but not surprised to recognize the man as one of the trustees from the center.

"How many in there with Maddie?" he asked.

"Just Mance."

"Give me the key to the apartment."

The man handed it over. "No need to look at me like that. I was made to—"

"Save it! Where's she holding Ms. McGuire?"

"She's in the bedroom. Mance is in the living room."

"You better not be lying," Riley said to the man in such a mordent tone that the guy actually quaked.

"I'm not. This isn't who I am. I had debts. I was coerced—"

"You're not just going to let yourself in, are you?" Copeland asked.

"Why not?" Riley shrugged. "She'll be expecting this punk. By the time she realizes her mistake, it'll be too late."

"You stay with him," Axel said to Copeland. "Riley and I have got this."

"You sure?"

Riley and Axel didn't bother to answer. Instead they made their way to the outside of 207 and waited. They couldn't hear any sounds from inside, but they hadn't expected to. Riley consulted his watch, both men focused on what they had to do. It was what they were trained for and what they did best. Implacably calm, Riley counted down the seconds, checked his weapon, and stood up. Motioning to Axel to take the opposite side of the door, he slid the key in the lock and kicked the door open wide.

Mance was seated on a ratty couch. So, too, was Maddie, and Mance's gun was held against the side of her forehead.

* * * *

"Did you think I was that stupid?" Mance asked, glaring at Riley.

"The thought crossed my mind."

"The bitch left a trail for you." Mance made a scoffing sound. "Thought I hadn't noticed."

"So now you're going to kill her?"

"I'm not a killer, but I *am* a survivor. Give me those papers and a head start and no one needs to get hurt. Otherwise…" She pressed the gun harder against Maddie's temple.

Riley scoffed. "Go right ahead and shoot. You won't get out of here alive if you do."

"I've seen the way you look at her," Mance replied. "You've got the hots for her real bad. You won't risk letting her die."

"Lady, I'm a Navy SEAL. We don't let personal feelings get in the way of duty." Riley and Axel both stood with their legs slightly apart and fixed her with steely gazes that made Maddie quake, even though they weren't directed at her. "Not ever."

"I am *not* going to face a court-martial," Mance replied. "But it doesn't need to come to that. Just give me those papers and let me out of here, that way everyone wins."

Riley shook his head. "Ain't gonna happen."

"What do you care about a few vets whose lives were finished anyway? They did some good on these drugs tests, helped speed things up. The FDA is so damned strict about stuff like that, you would not believe."

Mance was clearly losing patience. She was also as nervous as hell. Maddie could see that her forehead was dewy with perspiration, and the hand holding the gun was no longer quite so steady. Ranting on, like having two pissed-off SEALs in the room with their guns trained on her was no big deal, was a dead giveaway, too. She wasn't sure if that would make things easier for Riley or Axel or if it made Mance less predictable.

Hell, there had to be something she could do to move matters along. She wasn't just going to sit here placidly while a deranged woman used her for target practice. Maddie was beyond afraid. Of course she didn't want to die, but she'd kill Riley and Axel herself if they backed down for her sake. Not that they would, of course. Mance had got that bit entirely wrong. Neither of them had any particular feelings for her. Besides, this wasn't about her anymore. It was about finishing what her dad had started.

About making him proud of her, albeit posthumously.

Riley and Axel looked tough and determined, but she could see they were also frustrated. They desperately wanted to take Mance down but couldn't—not when she had her gun pointing straight at Maddie—the woman they'd been hired to protect. Presumably it was bad for business if they allowed clients to be blown away. A distraction was called for. They'd only need a second—or at least she damned well hoped that's all it would take—and Maddie had an idea. Mance's gun was no longer actually touching Maddie's head. Instead it was waving about just a fraction of an inch away from it.

It would have to be enough.

"Look, if you need me to *submit* to your plan," she said to Mance, emphasizing the key word and watching Riley in the periphery of her vision, "then I'm sure we can work something out."

She saw Riley incline his head, just fractionally, but it was enough for her to know he'd gotten the message.

"Submit!" Riley shouted into the ensuing silence.

"What the—"

Maddie threw herself sideways and instinctively covered her head with her hands. Two guns coughed twice each within a split second of one another, but Mance didn't appear to get off even a single shot. Cowering on the couch, Maddie saw Mance's body jerk with the impact of the bullets before it slumped onto Maddie, drenching her with blood. Mance had two neat holes in her forehead, a fraction of an inch apart, and two more on the left side of her chest.

"Maddie!"

Riley and Axel were beside her in seconds, pulling Mance off of her and checking her vital signs.

"She's gone," Axel said.

"Are you okay?" Riley asked, helping Maddie to sit up and examining her all over for signs of injury.

"Yes, I think so. Just give me a minute."

"Take all the time you need," Riley replied as Copeland and some of his men burst through the door, weapons drawn.

Now that it was all over, Maddie started to shake and couldn't seem to stop. Axel appeared with a cold cloth and wiped her face. Presumably she had Mance's blood on it. Riley then pulled her jacket off, which seemed to have taken the brunt of the blood. He removed his own leather jacket and draped it around her shoulders. It still retained his body warmth and smelled...well, masculine. It was comforting, as was the strong arm that circled her shoulders and held her close.

"I feel so damned stupid, not realizing it was her," Maddie muttered, fighting to stop her teeth from chattering.

"None of us knew," Axel said, moving in to kiss her forehead. "I'm just so damned proud of you for thinking up the *submit* plan."

"And for leaving the trail of beads," Riley added.

"I lost my mom's crystals," she said indignantly and then burst into tears.

Chapter Sixteen

"I was so damned scared," Maddie sobbed against Riley's shoulder.

"You were goddamned brave is what you were," he replied, brushing the hair off her face and kissing her, simply because he could.

"Thinking of the *submit* thing was genius," Axel added. "Not many people think so coherently in those sorts of situations."

Maddie pursed her lips. "I could sense she was nervous, I wasn't ready to die, so…"

"You created the opening we needed when I was all out of ideas." Riley stood up. "Come on, let's get out of here and leave Copeland to clear up."

"Won't they want to talk to us?"

"That can wait. We need to get you home."

"Glad to see you didn't forget anything you learned in your first sex lesson," Axel said. "I knew you were a good student, but really—"

Maddie managed a wan smile. "I needed something that would strike a chord with you. I figured that would do it."

"Count on it," Riley said, chuckling.

Axel drove while Riley cradled Maddie in his lap. She couldn't stop shaking but seemed to want to talk about what she'd been through.

"She was really afraid of the people she worked for," Maddie explained, choking on the words. "I think she'd gotten in too deep. She said it all started because she needed the money. Her mom was sick and couldn't pay her medical bills. Someone offered Mance a way out, and then she was stuck."

"Did she say who?" Axel asked.

"No, and I don't suppose it'll be easy to find out. These people hid themselves behind stooges like Mance."

"Where did you learn to use the word *stooge*?" Riley asked, smiling.

"I watch TV, just like everyone else. Anyway, I've earned the right to use any words I want."

"Damned straight," Axel agreed.

"She said she was done here but needed to make sure nothing in Dad's notes led back to the people controlling her. If that happened she said they'd come after her themselves."

"She doesn't need to worry about that now," Riley replied.

"I knew you needed a clear shot. She'd moved the gun away from me just a bit while you spoke to her, and so I—"

"Saved the day after we screwed up," Riley finished for her when she appeared too choked up to speak. "You're a heroine, darlin'. Your dad would be real proud."

"Do you really think so?" she asked in a tiny voice.

"I know it," he replied.

They arrived home and Riley carried Maddie through to the closest bathroom. He stripped off her soiled clothing while Axel set the shower running.

"Get yourself clean, honey," he said. "I'll wait right here."

She spent a long time in the shower, washing the smell of death from her skin. When she emerged Riley wrapped her in a huge fluffy towel and handed her a smaller one to wrap around her wet hair.

"Better?" he asked.

"Yes, a little."

"Come on. You need a hot drink."

In the kitchen, Axel had hot chocolate laced with brandy waiting for her. She obediently drank it all down, and Riley then suggested that she get some rest.

"I don't want to be alone," she said. "I'll have nightmares."

Given that she'd just seen a woman gunned down in front of her, Riley figured she was entitled to feel vulnerable.

"Come on," he said, sweeping her into his arms and carrying her through to the guest suite. "I guess we could all do with getting our heads down."

"Sorry about your crystals, darlin'," Axel said, following along.

"I was right about them," she said. "They were my lucky talisman. You never would have found me otherwise."

Axel pulled back the covers and Riley placed her beneath them. Both guys then shed their clothes and joined her, one on either side of her, intent upon keeping her safe while she slept. Riley knew she *was* safe now. It was over and she didn't actually need their protection. Nevertheless, they were there for her. There was bound to be a reaction to what she'd just seen. He slipped an arm around her shoulders and her head fell onto his chest like it belonged there. Axel's left arm spread over her stomach in a similarly possessive manner. The contact with them both appeared to sooth her because she fell asleep almost immediately.

* * * *

Maddie opened her eyes, thinking she'd probably slept for an hour or two, tops. Instead the sun was high in the sky, and glancing at the clock, she saw it was gone ten in the morning. She'd slept for twelve straight hours and felt rejuvenated. Better yet, she hadn't dreamt about the events of the previous day. Axel was beside her, eyes wide open, smiling at her.

"How you feeling?" he asked.

"Really rested." She frowned. "How did I sleep for so long?"

"That hot drink I gave you, I…er, put a little something in it besides brandy. I knew you wouldn't sleep otherwise but figured you'd object if I told you."

"You seem to know a lot about me."

"Darlin', you're human."

"Well, thanks. I think. Where's Riley?"

"Taking a call from Copeland. He wanted to come over and talk to you. Riley's putting him off until later."

As if on cue, Riley came back into the room.

"Hey, how you doin'?"

"I feel good, thanks. What did Copeland have to say for himself?"

"The guy who helped Mance is singing like a canary, but unfortunately he doesn't know much."

"So they'll get away with it?"

"Possibly. They're going through Mance's personal things with a fine-tooth comb, and if there's anything there, they'll find it. One thing's for sure, though. No more vets will be used for drugs tests. The word's being put out through the network, and everyone will know not to fall for it if the same thing is tried anywhere else in the country."

"That's something, I suppose," Maddie said, patting the empty space beside her. "Come back to bed."

"Something you ought to know," he said, perching on the edge of the bed. "We think your dad was run down in the narrow street behind the center. I'd been wondering about that. It's not easy to wait for someone to appear and then run them down as though by accident. But your dad would have needed to park in the garage and cross that quiet street to get to his car when he finished at the center. He was a man of regular habits, so they'd know when to expect him and could have been waiting."

"Oh." Maddie covered her mouth with her hand.

"Anyway," Riley continued, "I figured that had to be what happened. I told Copeland to ask Mance's sidekick about it, and I was right, although he claims not to know who drove the car."

"I see," Maddie said quietly. "Then they moved his body here and made it look as though he'd been hit while checking his mailbox."

"Right." Riley touched her cheek. "You okay?"

"Yes. I'm glad I know what happened."

"Copeland's coming to talk to us in an hour." Riley smiled at her. "I'll get breakfast going. I'm betting you're hungry."

"Actually, yes I am."

By the time Maddie had showered, dressed, and made her way to the kitchen, Riley had scrambled eggs and crispy bacon ready for them all, along with gallons of fresh coffee. Maddie hadn't touched the food at the center the previous day and was ravenous. She cleared her plate and then ate two slices of toast. She noticed the guys share an amused glance.

"What?" she demanded.

"Oh, nothing," Riley replied, chucking her chin. "Just glad to see you're not traumatized, is all."

"If I let what happen affect me then the bad guys win," she said with lofty scorn.

"Atagirl!"

Copeland arrived just after they'd cleared away the dishes.

"How are you, Ms. McGuire?" he asked.

"I'm hanging in there," Maddie replied, thinking Copeland had aged ten years in one day and didn't look as though he'd slept at all.

They spoke for an hour, asking as many questions as they answered. When they were all done, Copeland told them he'd need the three of them to come into the CIDC offices and make formal statements on Monday. To her shame, the first thought that went through Maddie's head was that Monday was two days away.

Two whole days in which to play with Riley and Axel.

"I expect you wanted to get away immediately," Maddie said to them after she'd shown Copeland out. "Will you mind hanging around for another two days?"

"Not at all," Riley replied. "In fact I was going to suggest that we helped you sort out the rest of your dad's things so you could leave as well if you want to, and get back to your life."

What life? "Yeah, if you're sure, that would be good. I've already spoken to the realtor, but—"

"We understand," Axel said. "Where do you want us to start?"

Maddie shared a glance between them and was overcome by a reckless desire to say what she was thinking. Without pausing to consider the wisdom of her whim, she came right out with it.

"How about with my next lesson?" she asked with a mischievous smile.

Riley blinked. "Come again?"

"I certainly plan to. You promised to teach me more stuff. Given how useful your first lesson proved to be in a life-and-death situation, I think you ought to deliver, don't you?"

"Yeah, but—"

"No buts and no strings," Maddie said firmly. "You owe me."

"I guess there's no arguing with that," Riley said, grinning. "Okay, babe, there's no time like the present. Go into the guest suite, take all your clothes off and stand in the corner, facing the wall until we're ready to join you."

It felt to Maddie as though her entire body flushed with anticipation and they hadn't laid so much as a finger on her yet.

"Yes, masters," she replied meekly, walking sedately away from them when what she really wanted to do was break the world sprinting record and get naked.

* * * *

"What are we supposed to make of that?" Axel asked as they watched her go.

"We've created a goddamned sex goddess," Riley replied, grinding his jaw.

"And that's a bad thing, because…"

"I didn't say it was a *bad* thing exactly."

"I know, she's different. Even Mance appeared to notice how you feel about her."

"She knew more than I do then," Riley said gruffly.

Axel grinned. "Have it your way. Come on, let's not keep a naked lady in need of punishment waiting."

"Talking of which, I visited the sex shop we saw on the edge of town."

"Ah, so that's the errand you had to run yesterday afternoon. I'd been meaning to ask." Axel flexed a brow and flashed a knowing smile. "Don't recall you making those sorts of deviations from jobs before."

"We've never fucked a client before." He shrugged. "You know me. I like to have the right stuff on hand." Riley reached into the closet where he'd left a carrier bag and tossed it at Axel. "There we go."

Axel delved into the bag and extracted nipple clamps, more lube, fluffy restraints, a Japanese flogger, and a butt plug.

"That ought to about cover it." Axel threw everything back into the bag and swung it by the handles. "Shall we?"

"After you."

They walked into the guest suite and found Maddie exactly where she was supposed to be—naked, standing in the corner with her head bowed. The sight of her cute butt caused lust to rip through Riley like a tornado, but he ignored his discomfort as they stood in the doorway and looked their fill. Her hair tumbled down her back and fell across her breasts, and she was trembling. Riley didn't think that was because she was cold. Neither one of them spoke. Instead they sat on the couch at the end of the bed and stripped off their clothes.

"Come here," Riley said once he was naked.

She turned slowly, flicked her hair over her shoulders, and walked toward them. When she was within range she stopped and lowered her eyes again. She is good at this, Riley thought, too damned good.

"Hold out your hands."

She did so and Riley attached the restraints. With her wrists cuffed, she dropped her hands so they covered her pussy, again not looking directly at them. Riley could see moisture trickling from her cunt and working its way down her inner thigh. He tamped down the desire to lick it away. First, she needed to be punished. Without saying a word he worked lube into her solidified nipples and then attached the clamps. She gasped and clearly wanted to speak, but didn't. The minx had so far avoided giving them any reasons to chastise her, seeming to understand this game even though they hadn't bothered to explain the rules to her.

Shit, there were no rules!

Riley stood up and positioned a footstool just in front of them.

"On your knees," he said to Maddie. "Lean over that so your gut's on the middle and your tits dangle the other side."

She got into position and remained perfectly still. Once again Riley and Axel took a moment to admire the view. She'd knelt with her legs slightly apart, giving them a clear view of both her ass and the lush pink lips of her pussy. It was just about the prettiest damned view either of them had seen for a long while.

"Would you like to teach her some respect?" Riley asked Axel.

"Someone needs to," he replied, taking the flogger from Riley and standing up.

"Axel's gonna flog your sweet ass, darlin'," Riley told her. "Just remember your breathing, like we did with the tantric thing, and wait for the pain to become pleasurable. Having the clamps on your tits will help. They restrict the blood flow and make them more sensitive."

She nodded and Axel went to work. He spread one large hand over her ass and then rested the thongs of the flogger on it, getting her used to the feel of them. Then he lifted the weapon and brought it down lightly. She grunted but held her position.

"Okay?" Axel asked.

She nodded, so he repeated the process a little harder. Riley noticed that her juices had reached almost to her knees. She was loving this. Axel continued with the punishment for a minute or two more, putting a little more force behind each blow.

"That'll do for starters," Riley said. "Have you learned your lesson, Maddie?"

"I'm not sure," she replied from beneath the curtain of her hair. "Can you repeat the question please?"

Both men stifled laughs as Riley walked up to her. If he didn't touch every inch of her pretty damned soon, he'd disgrace himself by shooting his load then and there. That was the power she had over him, yet *she* was the one wearing the restraints and being flogged. Riley figured she probably knew she was the one in control. She'd reduced two badass SEALs to quivering wrecks and was enjoying every damned minute of it. There was something about Maddie that got to Riley on all levels. If things were different...Damn it, how often had that thought gone through his head these past few days?

Get over yourself.

Riley's hands took their turn to move over her ass. Its cheeks were now striped pink from the flogging she'd just taken, and Riley rubbed lube over them so gently that she probably barely felt it. But she definitely reacted when his finger rimmed her anus and slid smoothly inside.

"Just relax for me, darlin'," he said, "and let me do my work."

Her coiled muscles because a little less taut and he slid a second finger inside, moving them slowly, getting her used to the sensation.

"That's it, sugar. Let me inside. This is gonna blow your mind."

She mumbled something incomprehensible, appearing to be completely with the program. Riley removed his fingers and replaced them with the tip of the plug that Axel had already lubed.

"This is gonna distend you, darlin'," he said, sliding a little bit more of it into her. "Make you ready for our cocks. You okay with that?"

"Yes," she said breathlessly. "It feels kinda invasive but nice, if that makes sense."

"Perfect sense," Riley replied, slipping the plug all the way home.

He left her crouched over the stool and leaned over her, completely covering her with his body heat as his hands sought out her clamped nipples. He gently tugged on the chain that connected them and she cried out.

"Did that hurt?"

"Hell, no!"

Both men laughed. "Just checking," Riley said, rubbing his rigid cock down the crack in her ass. "Wouldn't want to hurt you now, would we, sugar."

He pushed her hair aside and nuzzled her neck, biting his way down its long column and then retracing his steps so he could suck one entire earlobe into his mouth. She shuddered and pushed back against him, her skin slick with perspiration, her breathing short and increasingly desperate. She was ready for him.

Riley removed the plug. It slipped out with a slick popping sound and fell onto the floor. Before she had a chance to miss it, Riley slipped the tip of his cock into its place. She gasped.

"You're too big," she said.

"That's an awfully nice compliment, darlin'," he said in a throaty drawl, "but unfortunately not true. Just relax and trust me. You took it once before."

"You feel bigger today."

"Nah, I'm just the same."

Riley needed to take care and move slowly. Only problem was, he was on sensory overload, and moving slowly would be a challenge. The musky scent of her arousal was driving him wild. So, too, was her willingness to do this just hours after being held hostage and seeing a woman shot dead in front of her. Grunting with the effort it took him to be slow and precise, Riley inched his way a little deeper.

"How does that feel?" he asked.

"Hmm, I'm not sure."

"Witch!"

Riley leaned forward to nip at her shoulder blade as he withdrew almost all the way and then sank back into her. This time she pushed back against him, making cute groaning noises as she took him inside.

"Let me do the work, babe," he said. "Don't wanna hurt you."

"You'll hurt me more by holding back," she panted.

Axel chuckled. They both ignored him as Riley got down to business and his thick heat completely filled her backside. Something strange was going on—a feeling he'd hadn't known since... *Hell, don't go there.* Too late for that. The draw Riley felt toward this feisty, high-spirited lady tugged at him on a level he had no control over. Straining not to explode, his emotions were as overloaded as his cock and he knew he wouldn't be able to last much longer. His balls had already pulled tighter and he felt the rush building, rapidly slipping past his self-control. He moved one hand around her side and played with her clit.

"Let's do this," he said, withdrawing and then sliding deeper than before.

"Yes," she said. "It feels astonishing. I think, I can't... Shit, I'm going to come."

And she did. That's one of the things he loved about her. She wasn't afraid to express her feelings and to go with them. Riley closed his eyes, fucking her until her spasming body finally stopped moving and she expelled a deep sigh of contentment. Then he took his turn.

His loaded balls slapped painfully against her buttocks as he drove into her and let himself go.

"Yesss!" he said, throwing his head back and howling like a wolf.

Only as he slid out of her and fell, exhausted, onto the rug did it occur to him that he'd used the *L* word, if only inside his head.

What the fuck…Riley had only ever loved one woman in his entire life. Hadn't he?

Chapter Seventeen

Axel fetched a washcloth and cleaned Maddie up. Riley headed for the bathroom and dealt with his own needs.

"You all right, darlin'?" Axel asked her, helping her to her feet.

Her eyes were sparkling, and she had a look of deep satisfaction about her that Axel loved seeing.

"Come and lie down, take a moment and get your breath back."

He took her hand and led her to the bed.

"But I'm not breathless." She ran her fingers through the hairs on his chest. "I want to play some more."

"Is that right?"

"Uh-huh."

"What do you wanna do?"

"That's not for me to say."

Axel was having trouble believing what he was hearing. She'd just taken Riley's huge length up her ass and was already after more. This chick blew his mind, and then some! Leaving her was gonna be one hell of a wrench. *Admit it, you don't wanna leave her.*

"Okay then, babe, let's see if we can find somewhere to put this." Axel fisted his rigid cock. "Any thoughts?"

She chuckled. "My thoughts would probably get me arrested."

"Well, we can't have that, can we now."

Axel sat up, pulled her into his arms, and then lay down again, tumbling her on top of him so that her clamped tits landed just above his lips, right where he wanted them to be. She still wore the restraints and rested her elbows on either side of his face, looking down at him with a question in her eye and laughter on her lips. Damn it, she was making him feel stuff he didn't want to feel. Sex was just a means to an end. Emotion didn't have any place in it.

Axel held her in place with one hand while lathing first one nipple and then the other with his tongue. She made a purring sound at the back of her throat when his erection popped up between her legs. She closed them greedily around it like she never planned to let it go. Axel could live with that thought. Hell, this babe was one in a million. He and Riley would be idiots to let her go. But the alternative was unthinkable, wasn't it? It would change just about everything in their lives, and in hers, too. That was even supposing she'd be willing.

Or if Riley would.

Axel shook his head to dispel such thoughts and concentrated on the job at hand. He noticed Riley reemerge from the bathroom and pick up the flogger. Axel understood why. Leaning over Axel, Maddie's butt would be sticking up in the air, way too cute to resist. Riley brought the flogger gently down over it without warning her to expect it. She jerked but didn't seem unduly concerned. Shit, was she a natural sub, or what? Axel guided the head of his cock to her entrance and thrust into her with one powerful lift of his hips, stretching her to the limit, filling her with his throbbing member. Axel's entry coincided with a harder crack of the flogger, causing her to draw in a sharp breath and gasp.

"Okay?" he asked.

"Wonderful!" She sank down on him with all her weight and closed the muscles in her vagina around him as though she was worried he might change his mind. *As if!*

Axel upped the pace of his thrusts. Riley, breathing hard, continued to thrash her butt as Axel tugged on the chain linking the nipple clamps. Maddie's eyes were wide open as she absorbed the pleasure and pain they strove to create.

"I have to tell you that I'm on the edge," she said on an apologetic note. "I guess you want it to last, but…shit, Axel, fuck me!"

"My pleasure, sugar."

He rammed himself into her, his cock expanding as her pleasure communicated itself. As he embedded deep inside her, fucking her brains out while Riley flogged her ass, Maddie went completely wild. She rode him like a woman on a mission, and Axel loved the way she left herself go with such total abandonment. She threw her head back and screamed at the rafters, thrashing about with no real sense of rhythm, taking what she so obviously needed with greedy disregard for his diminishing self-control.

Axel gave her a moment to regain her breath and then turned over. They were still joined and she rolled with him, finishing up underneath.

"Legs round my neck," he said curtly. "I need to get deeper."

Riley threw a couple of pillows beneath her butt so Axel could get the angle he needed to ease his ache. An ache that had never been more persistent or urgent. He pounded into her, hard and fast. She moved with him, encouraging him with throaty moans until the flickering heat inside him turned into a raging inferno. The sensation burned as he teetered on the brink of something remarkable.

"Here it comes." Axel closed his eyes and thrust as hard and deep as he could. "That's it, babe, now you've got me."

She closed her silken fist around him and cried out as she came for a second time. He pulsated as together they flew to a higher plane and she drained him completely dry.

* * * *

Is this for real? Maddie wondered, dozing between the two guys after her session with Axel. What they'd done for her was beyond amazing. She felt rejuvenated, renewed, ready to conquer the world. Then she remembered they'd be gone in a couple of days and came crashing back to earth with a resounding thump. Talk about a passion killer.

Don't think that way, Maddie. Live for the moment.

"You okay?" Riley asked, leaning up on one elbow and examining her face.

"Why wouldn't I be?" she replied, biting her lower lip to stop herself from grinning. "You guys were, er…adequate."

"Adequate!" Axel sat up and tapped her thigh. "Someone's asking to be chastised."

"Ah, he catches on."

She saw them exchange a glance and then laugh.

"Calling a man's performance adequate will get you more than a chastisement, darlin'," Riley drawled. "It's downright insulting."

"Oh, sorry. Is it?"

"Honey, we'll give you whatever you want, but what we won't do is move too fast. You've only just started on anal sex. It takes time to get used to it."

Time was what they didn't have, but if she reminded them of that, they might think she was hinting about something more permanent.

"I'm good with it," she said, wishing she knew how to flutter her lashes like she'd seen other women do. "What happens next?"

Another look passed over her head.

"We kinda thought you'd need some downtime, honey," Axel said. "We're not animals."

"Oh, I don't know."

"Maddie!" Riley's handsome faced hovered inches above hers. "Be serious."

"I was." She reached for the finger he wagged beneath her nose and sucked it into her mouth. "Come on, guys, time for my next lesson. Or aren't you…er, *up* for it?"

Before she knew what was happening, a strong pair of arms plucked her from the bed and she found herself facedown over an equally strong pair of thighs. Whose? Riley had a mole halfway up his right thigh, so it had to be him. His hand came down heavily on her backside without warning. Even so, she'd been expecting it and absorbed the pain with gladness in her heart.

"Get those damned restraints again, Axel," he said, spanking her a little harder. "We'll show her what we're up for."

Riley tilted her upright and Axel reaffixed the restraints.

"Lie on your back and raise your arms above your head, sugar," Riley said.

She did so, and Axel somehow attached the chain between the restraints to the headboard. Then her world went dark when Riley placed a blindfold over her eyes. She hoped the nipple clamps would come back into play as well, but that didn't happen. She wanted to ask why not but resisted. Presumably they had other plans for her.

Sure enough, she felt two pairs of hands rubbing some sort of fragrant lotion into her body, but only after they'd explored every nook and cranny with their lips, tongues, and teeth. She never knew where she'd be sucked or nipped next, and the sensation was driving her wild. She was probably supposed to remain passive, but that was beyond her. It would be beyond anyone because they'd brought her to the pinnacle of need again. Raw desire washed through her, and her turbulent emotions had gone off the scale.

"Please!"

She hadn't meant to say the word aloud, afraid that begging might cause them to tease her by stopping what they were doing. Instead a hand pushed her onto her side and a finger played with her anus. At the same time a pair of lips clamped onto a nipple and sucked. Hard. Maddie cried out. Not being able to see or use her hands made her feel totally helpless, adding to the sensual nature of the game because she was forced to place her trust in them. And she did trust them.

Absolutely.

She couldn't believe how badly she needed to be fucked, having only just finished with Axel. She'd never been that into sex before, but these two had well and truly tempted her appetite. That being so, she intended to make the most of them before they left.

Don't think about them leaving. Live for the moment, remember?

The lips left her nipple, the finger left her butt, and a moan of protest left Maddie's lips.

"Get on your knees and support your weight on your elbows," Riley's voice instructed.

She tried to do as she was told and collided with a solid body. Hands helped her into a position directly over that body. It was Riley, she thought, because she recognized his deep chuckle when her knee collided clumsily with his rigid cock.

The mattress dipped behind her. Axel had presumably climbed onto it, and it was him nipping playfully at her ass. Riley's fingers parted her slick folds and then the tip of his cock penetrated her. At the same time, Axel's head slid into her backside. Shit, they were going to fuck her at the same time! Was she ready for this? She only had to say and they'd stop, she knew that, but did she want them to?

"All right?" Riley's voice asked, as though sensing her hesitation.

"Yes," she said after a slight pause. "Absolutely. Let's do it."

"Okay, darlin'," Riley said. "Keep absolutely still and let us do all the work."

"Yes, I can do that."

"I know you can."

They started to move in tandem. Axel worked his way into her butt as Riley withdrew from her pussy, presumably to make room for him. Then the position reversed. A disturbing thrill jolted her, both as a result of what they were doing and the helplessness of her position. She could hear their heavy breathing and her own needy little moans as they plundered her body, bringing her alive in ways she'd never dreamed were possible. She felt Axel's hot breath on the damp skin of her back, Riley's fingers probing between them to seek out her clit, Axel's balls thumping against her buttocks, the abrasive rub of the hairs on Riley's chest against her sensitized tits. The combination was too much for her. She didn't know where they found their self-restraint because she didn't have any and was going to come already.

Liquid heat flowed through her veins as the feeling intensified and her body coursed with readiness. Again.

"Guys, I'm gonna come. I'm so damned close."

"You are *not* going to come until we say you can," Riley's voice admonished.

"But I need to…I can't…"

"If you come, there will be consequences."

"Okay but…Oh, shit!"

Maddie screamed. Her breathing fractured, she forgot all about remaining still and pushed herself against first one thick cock and then the other, wondering if her overstimulated heart could withstand so much pleasure. She screwed her eyes tightly shut and rode her orgasm as her spirit soared and her body drifted into exquisite oblivion.

"We told you not to do that," Axel said when she came back down to earth.

"You'll have to pay for your disobedience, babe," Riley added, laughter in his voice.

"I'll take my punishment like a man," she said meekly.

"Ain't nothing masculine about you, babe," Axel said, picking up the pace again.

She couldn't believe it. This should be their turn, she'd just had, was it her third or fourth orgasm within an hour, and yet she could feel another building?

"Come on, darlin'," Riley said, thrusting himself hard into her cunt.

"How did you know?" she asked breathlessly.

"We know," they said together, tension in their voices, presumably because they were finally letting themselves get close.

Maddie wasn't about to miss out. She surrendered herself to their cocks and felt a different sort of heat infuse her body this time. It came from deep within her core and spread more slowly yet more deeply to the outermost reaches of her extremities before taking root in her gut and then lower.

"Let's do this together," Axel said, his voice strained.

"I hear you," Riley said, giving an almighty thrust that sent Maddie toppling over the abyss.

Riley tensed and then grunted. Axel did the same, and all three of them were lost in the erotic maze of a mind-blowing orgasm that for Maddie eclipsed everything that had gone before.

Chapter Eighteen

No sorting out of her father's possessions got done that weekend. The three of them spent their time in bed, eating or sleeping. Maddie didn't care about her father's things. She was in seventh heaven and refused to think beyond the here and now.

In spite of her efforts to hold back time, Monday morning eventually arrived and they spent most of the day at CIDC headquarters, making official statements, going over and over the same ground. By the time they returned home Maddie was beat and excused herself. She absolutely had to close her eyes for a few minutes. She didn't really want to waste a moment more than necessary away from the guys. There would be plenty of time for sleeping once they were gone. They ought to be gone already, but events had taken longer than expected today and it was too late for them to go now, so they got to have another night together.

The bonus was a gift from heaven, so she wouldn't waste it by resting for long. Axel said he'd sent out for something to eat, and she was hungry—in all senses of the word. She didn't know when she'd changed into a sex maniac, nor did she much care. Better late than never, and she had lost time to make up for.

Yawning, she fell out of bed, pulled an oversized T-shirt over her nakedness, and wandered toward the kitchen. Slightly raised voices—Riley's and Axel's slightly raised voices—caused her to pause in the passageway. What were they arguing about? She didn't want any discord on their final day together. Curiosity and fear mingled inside her as she heard her name mentioned, causing her to shamelessly eavesdrop.

"Admit it, buddy," Axel said. "She's got to you, just like she has me."

"You think?" Riley replied caustically.

"I know it, and so do you. The question is, what do you plan to do about it?"

"What can I do?"

"Oh, for God's sake!"

"Axel, do what you gotta do. If you want Maddie then go for it. If she's willing to move to Chesapeake then that'll be cool. You and I can still run our business there, and I can get Raoul to assign me another partner."

"Ain't gonna happen, buddy."

"Now who's got hang-ups?"

Maddie leaned against the wall, listening to their argument going back and forth like a fast-moving tennis ball. Her heart lifted and she felt more empowered with each word they spoke. She fallen deeply and passionately in love with both of them but figured her feelings weren't reciprocated so was willing to behave like a grown-up and let them go without making a fuss. Now she knew differently, and she was damned if the best thing that had ever happened to her would slip through her fingers. She was through with living her life on other people's terms. It was time to stand up for what she wanted.

She waited until Riley embarked on a long list of reasons why they needed to get the hell out of Dodge and then stepped into the room. Both men abruptly stopped yelling and faced her with sheepish expressions.

"Er, sorry," Riley said. "We didn't know you were there."

"Obviously."

She sauntered up to the breakfast bar and took the stool opposite theirs. They were clearly embarrassed, but she noticed both of them checking out her thighs as she sat down and her T-shirt rode up. The gesture gave her confidence, but she didn't speak, waiting for one of them to say something first. When they didn't, she took matters into her own hands.

"You know, I've heard SEALs described as many things," she said in a conversational tone, "but never cowards."

Both men tensed. "Wadda you mean?" Riley asked.

"What I said. You're a coward, Riley Maddox, and so are you, Axel Cameron."

"Careful," Riley warned.

"Why? Does the truth hurt? There's something you want, which would be me for what I just overheard, but you're scared to go for it in case you get hurt." She shrugged. "Sounds pretty cowardly to me."

"You don't understand."

"Really? What I understand is that Axel had more responsibility thrust upon him than any sixteen-year-old should ever have to shoulder. At a time when he should have been smoking pot, cutting classes, and chasing girls, he was holding down two jobs and praying the authorities wouldn't catch him caring for his siblings and break the family up." She looked at Axel and her voice softened. "That's enough to put anyone off commitment for life. I understand that. But just because you love someone and want to commit to them, it doesn't mean your freedom has to be curtailed. If we were together, no way would I let you stop working for Raoul."

"But the danger?"

"Life's full of dangers. Sometimes you just have to take a chance if there's something you want badly enough." She turned to face Riley. "And as for you. Where to start? You loved your wife, I get that bit, really I do, and she was taken from you. That sucks, but so does life. Given what you do for a living, you ought to know that better than most people. Do you really think Stella wouldn't want you to be happy again?"

Riley looked too stunned to speak. "The pain," he muttered. "I couldn't go through that again. I couldn't risk you getting drawn into all our shit."

"So you'd deny yourself?"

"You don't understand."

Maddie lost it at that point. Too agitated to remain passive, she stood up and got right in his face. "Is that right? You think I haven't had my share of hardships? You think commitment doesn't scare the heck out of me as well?" She shook her head. "You guys kept asking me about my past, and I wouldn't tell you. Well, I'm ready to tell you now. You know what it's like being an army brat, being moved from place to place, never having time to make proper friends before you move on." Both men's gazes were locked on her face and they nodded in unison. "My parents became my best friends because I didn't really have anyone else. I loved them both but was closer to my dad and did everything in my power to make him proud of me."

"I'm sure he was," Axel said quietly.

"And I'm sure of no such thing. He was married to my mother and then the army in that order. There wasn't room for anyone else in his life."

"But I thought—" Riley shook his head. "I thought you and he were close."

"We became closer these last few years, after Mom passed and he left the army. Before that, everything I tried to do to win his approval was never good enough. If I got an A in a test, it ought to have been an A-plus. If I played tennis and got to a final, I ought to have won, and…well, you get the picture."

"He was an overachiever," Riley said.

"And then some. I never stopped trying to win his approval and never quite managed it. That's why, when he tried to get me together with a young captain he approved of, I took up with the guy, even though I didn't like him much." She paused. "It was the first and only time I saw the approval in his eye that I so craved."

"What happened to the captain?" Riley asked, scowling.

"Before or after he put me in the hospital for the third time?"

Both men leapt from their seats. "He abused you?" Axel asked, murder in his eyes.

"Yeah, Dad's perfect officer was a bully and a tyrant but knew how to hide it and turn on the charm when there was someone he wanted to impress and who could help his career, like my dad."

"How long did you stay with him?" Riley asked, clenching his fists. "And more to the point, why did you?"

"Almost a year, and I stayed, obviously, to get that parental approval I craved. Besides, he was always sorry when he hit me. It would never happen again."

Riley glowered at the wall. "That's what they all say."

"And you let us spank you?" Axel frowned. "Didn't it freak you out?"

"Did I appear freaked?"

"Well no, but—"

"What we did was consensual. For mutual pleasure. There's a huge difference." She paused. "Besides, what would you have done if you'd known?"

"Not what we did, that's for sure," Riley said.

"Precisely why I didn't tell you. I wanted to try what you were offering."

"Okay," Riley said. "We'll talk about that later. Tell me more about your lousy captain."

"Not much to tell. In the end I called a halt and moved to New York, where I could lose myself in the city. I'd accepted by then that I'd never do anything to win Dad's approval and that I'd just have to get over it." She paused. "But then this. At least I managed to get to the bottom of the business at the center, with your help."

"Honey," Riley said, running a hand through his hair.

"Don't you dare 'honey' me!" She stood directly in front of him, hands on hips, like a prize fighter. "I'm prepared to put all that crap behind me and make a commitment. Does the prospect scare me? Bet your life it does, but there are no guarantees in this world, and what's more, it ain't a dress rehearsal. Far as I know, we only get one shot at it." She glanced at Axel. "And being with you guys has brought me truly alive. It's made me want to take a chance again, but if you're too lily-livered to risk it, then—"

"You have a life and career in New York," Riley said, a fledgling smile breaking through his stern expression.

"Don't they have houses that need makeovers up there?"

"Only about a thousand of them," Axel replied, taking her hand.

"And you could start with ours," Riley said, taking her other hand and raising it to his lips. "Oh, and while I think of it, I have something for you."

He picked up a package from the table and handed it to her. Maddie opened it and gasped.

"My crystals," she said. "You had them collected and restrung."

Axel shrugged. "As many as we could find. You said they had sentimental value."

"How can I ever thank you?"

"Why don't we spend the next few decades trying to decide," Riley said, swooping in for a kiss. Maddie held him off.

"What are you saying?" she asked.

"I'm trying to say that you're right. It's time to make a commitment. And just so that you know, we're not cowards. We just hadn't found the right woman to love, and share." Riley's eyes glowed like molten lava as he concentrated them on her face. "Now we have and it's time to start living again."

Maddie flashed a radiant smile and hugged each of them in turn. "I love you both, too," she said, finally allowing herself to be kissed.

Epilogue

"Hot damn, I don't believe it." Raoul leaned back in his chair and stared at his computer screen.

"What don't you believe?" Zeke asked.

"Come see for yourself."

Zeke leaned over Raoul's shoulder and read the e-mail that Raoul didn't believe.

"Riley and Axel have hooked up with Maddie McGuire." Zeke shook his head. "Now I really do believe in miracles."

"I thought those two were an emotion-free zone."

Zeke shot him a look. "Takes one to know one."

"Don't go there!"

"Just sayin'." Zeke's smile faded. "But you ought to follow their example and at least think about it, buddy. Can't go on living in the past forever."

"Why not? You do."

"Only to keep you company."

"I'm glad the guys have found someone," Raoul said, not wanting to go where Zeke was trying to take this conversation. "And they still wanna work with us. That's good. They'd be tough to replace."

"They did well down there, sorting out that drugs scam. I'm surprised it hasn't hit the news though, a big scandal like that."

"A lot of people have good reason to keep it quiet, including the military, seeing as how one of their own was involved. You know how good they are at keeping these things in-house."

Zeke rolled his eyes. "Yeah, don't I just."

Raoul swung his feet off his desk and stood up. "Anyway, perhaps we'll take a weekend at Chesapeake once the guys are settled, and live the good life vicariously."

Zeke chuckled. "If I didn't know better, I'd say you were jealous."

"Good job you know better then."

"Yeah." Zeke sighed as he watched Raoul leave the room. "Ain't it just."

THE END

ABOUT THE AUTHOR

Zara Chase is a British author who spends a lot of her time travelling the world. Being a gypsy provides her with ample opportunities to scope out exotic locations for her stories. She likes to involve her heroines in her erotic novels in all sorts of dangerous situations—and not only with the hunky heroes whom they encounter along the way. Murder, blackmail, kidnapping, and fraud—to name just a few of life's more common crimes—make frequent appearances in her books, adding pace and excitement to her racy stories.

Zara is an animal lover who enjoys keeping fit and is on a one-woman mission to keep the wine industry ahead of the recession.

www.zarachase.com

For all titles by Zara Chase, please visit
www.bookstrand.com/zara-chase

Siren Publishing, Inc.
www.SirenPublishing.com

Lightning Source UK Ltd.
Milton Keynes UK
UKOW03f2111141013

219063UK00021B/1996/P